TITANS

CAPTIVATED

THEIRS TO LOVE

ENTICING BILLIONAIRES

SIERRA CARTWRIGHT

USA TODAY BESTSELLING AUTHOR

DEDICATION

For Team Can-Do for saying, I've got you. I see you. I appreciate you. Bev, GG, Cassie, Linda. And especially Shan, I'm sending you all the snacks you want!

CHAPTER ONE

Energy leashed, but barely, Drake Griffin paced the confines of the conference room on the second floor of the Braes, an ultraprivate club owned by the Zeta Society. The unobtrusive building, set behind iron gates, was in an exclusive area of Houston. It was a place where high-stakes deals were negotiated and signed.

He would know. He'd inked plenty of deals inside these hallowed walls.

As one of the city's boldest hotshot lawyers, he'd outmaneuvered even the best of the best on behalf of his clients.

Yeah, he was a cutthroat. Though he wasn't widely liked, he was respected, and he'd take that above warm and fuzzy feels all day, every day.

Tonight, though, mattered more than any other deal he'd been involved in. This time, he had something personal at stake. Not just a shitpile of old family money but also his reputation.

After tonight, his star would be forever hitched to Everett Parker's.

At one time, they'd been more than acquaintances. Drake considered the other man to be among his small circle of friends. They'd golfed together, shot hoops on the weekend, bounced ideas off each other. And they'd discovered they shared an interest in BDSM. Since they both appreciated the same type of submissive—dark haired, beautiful, and curvy—they'd occasionally teamed up to Top the same woman.

Now Parker despised him. Not that Drake blamed him.

He'd been the one responsible for knocking the king-maker off his lofty and laudable perch. Until Drake came along, Parker had enjoyed a ridiculously long run of success. His uncanny knack for predicting political winners had earned him the nickname of the Oracle. In a short amount of time, he'd gotten a supreme court justice through the nomination process, managed to get several members of the president's cabinet confirmed, and helped elect a US senator and dozens of House members. Not to mention the way he'd stacked the state legislature in favor of the governor.

Then Bob Finglas, candidate for office, had hired Drake to lead his opposition research team.

For at least the tenth time, he checked the face of his high-tech watch. The digits changed to 9:01 p.m. Which meant Parker was late.

No call. No explanation.

As someone who billed by the minute, Drake's time was, quite literally, money. Since the two had met in person no less than a dozen times to hammer out every single detail, Everett knew Drake despised tardiness. The slight was no doubt meant to tug on Drake's temper—something that was never very far beneath the surface.

Needing to take the edge off his growing frustration, he glanced at the very expensive bottle of whiskey and two glasses on the sideboard. A gift from Julien Bonds. It was meant to be opened after Everett and Drake signed the thick pile of papers in the middle of the long, polished table. The fact they had to meet at the club—neutral ground—rather than in one of their offices, said a lot about each man's reluctance to yield power.

But Bonds thought a partnership between the two men was a brilliant idea. And the Genius almost always got what he wanted.

Almost?

Right.

Julien Bonds got whatever the hell he wanted—fuck the very real consequences. And in this case, Drake was certain that meant his sanity.

9:02.

He stopped pacing and dragged his hand through his hair, dislodging a lock that fell across his forehead. At five after, he'd say fuck it all. If Parker couldn't even fucking be bothered to show up, Drake would grab the luxury single malt and exit the building. He'd tell Bonds to send the bill to Parker.

With twenty-seven seconds remaining, Parker pushed open the door. "Evening, Griffin."

No acknowledgement of his lateness and certainly no apology.

Not that Drake expected one.

More because decorum dictated than any real congeniality, the two shook hands. Both men were wearing rings that signified they belonged to the Zetas, a secret society. Members were often referred to as Titans. The ranks were comprised of world leaders, Pulitzer Prize winning authors, famous playwrights, scientists, researchers, futurists, politicians, doctors, lawyers, judges, and most of the richest people on the planet. Their symbol was Athena's owl, and emeralds served as the talisman's eyes. And now the gems flashed in the bright overhead lighting. "You're late."

Ignoring the comment, Everett glanced around the room, taking in the two chairs that Drake had placed across from each other, the stack of legal paperwork, the closed blinds, and then the whiskey bottle with a bow on top. "Bonds?"

"None other."

"Optimistic bastard."

Seemed Drake and Everett had finally found something they agreed on.

Without taking a seat, Everett dragged the manila folder toward him and flipped it open.

"Everything is in order." Of course it was. A legal hound through and through, he'd personally overseen every fucking one of the billion details. And there'd been a fucking pile of them. Months' worth.

Distrust tattooed in Everett's eyes, he looked up. Maybe because his suit was black or a trick of the lighting, his eyes seemed dark, more gray than blue. "I'll see for myself."

Drake strode to the back of the room where the staff had provided coffee service, a charcuterie board, sodas, and a carafe filled with water. Fruits and veggies floated on the top. Who the hell needed cucumber in their drink?

He opened the small refrigerator and found an energy drink. Much better. He needed to remain sharp. The way Everett was reading each page, the night promised to be long.

"I'll have coffee." Everett glanced up. "Thanks."

Screw you. Drake hadn't offered. This meeting was getting worse by the minute. "Didn't you read the files Smytherson sent over?" One of Bonds's most trusted advisers. Someone both he and Everett had agreed on.

"I did."

The words hung in the air. They weren't an accusation exactly but close enough. "Look, Parker—"

"Might as well get comfortable." Everett shrugged out of his jacket and hung it on the back of a chair. "I plan to."

Fuck. He'd been hoping to go to the Retreat, a nearby BDSM club, at some point this evening.

After taking a seat, Everett picked up the first page.

Because he was anxious to get back to his real life and have this in his rearview mirror, Drake actually poured his would-be partner a cup of the rich, strong-smelling brew.

"A splash of cream, if you don't mind."

Drake clenched his back teeth. If this deal didn't get done soon, he'd need to see a dentist.

Everett barely looked up when Drake delivered the beverage. Instead of taking a drink, he slid the cup and saucer to one side and continued to read while Drake paced.

Half an hour later, Parker took a break to remove his cufflinks. The gold clanked against the wood, the sound seeming to reverberate off the walls. Then he turned back his shirtsleeves.

"For fuck's sake." His hold on his temper finally fracturing, Drake shoved a chair into the table. "Not a word has changed since you last read the document. And you goddamn well know it."

Somehow Parker managed to raise a single eyebrow.

"Look…" Drake sighed in frustration. How he wished he'd dropped in to the Braes's fitness center before the meeting. He'd have been less agitated if he'd burned off some of his excess energy. But as always, his schedule had been packed, and today he'd started an hour before dawn.

In the years since he'd taken down Parker, they'd never discussed what had happened. "Think what you will. I've never been dishonest in my dealings with you."

"You want to go there?"

The animosity between them was as thick as it was seemingly insurmountable. "Maybe we should." For better or worse.

"You could have given us a heads-up."

"And give the kingmaker the opportunity to convince me to bury the information for the greater good?" Whatever the hell that even was anymore. At one time, he might have been young enough, idealistic enough, to believe in some higher good. "Politics is a dirty and dangerous game." Parker knew it better than Drake did. "I did my job."

"All's fair?"

"You'd have done the same fucking thing."

"Would I?"

Dripping with meaning, with accusation, the frigid question hung in the air.

Everett slid the untouched coffee to one side and returned to his reading.

"Call me when you're done."

"You're sure I won't make any addendums?"

"Fuck, Parker. Is our entire partnership going to be like this? We have to be able to trust one another."

"At one time, I trusted you."

"Look—" *Damn it.* Drake had wanted tonight to be a new start. But without addressing the past, was that even possible?

Everett sat back and pressed his palms together. In thought? Judgment?

"Do you want an apology?"

"Since you don't see that you did anything wrong, no."

"Employing trackers is as old as time." Meaning Drake had directed the campaign to hire people to follow Everett's candidate around twenty-four seven and note her every move.

"It is." Everett tilted his head to one side in acknowledgment. "But not when you were once an advisor to Allison's campaign."

"I helped you vet her before her first term. Not the same thing."

"You knew our strategies, her weaknesses. You went to great lengths to point them out."

That much was true, and something he was good at. It helped him shore up his clients more than once.

But when it came to Allison Danbury, no one would have guessed the sitting senator would be caught in a compromising position with a male staffer half her age—one who'd dated her daughter.

When an anonymous tip had been sent to Drake, he dismissed it. The Allison he knew prized her family above anything else.

"You're good at what you do. The best, as Bonds says. But there's a reason not a lot of people like you."

Drake had never been burdened by the need for anyone's approval. "If it hadn't been me, it would have been someone else."

"Maybe. The fact is, you knew my playbook and how to deploy the information."

He shrugged. "Parts of it. Not the entire thing." But the Finglas media team had done an exceptional job of deploying the intel in the most effective ways possible.

Scandalicious—an online news/gossip site—broke the news twelve hours before early voting started, which meant it would steal headlines across Danbury's district.

Every day, more salacious details were dripped.

Because Parker had been in control, spinning the story as only he could, she'd responded with class and dignity, all the right words, and heartfelt remorse. Shockingly Allison's early-return numbers were higher than expected. Her team, including her husband, planned a hell of a party to celebrate her victory. Everything crashed around them as results from the outlying precincts trickled in.

"At best your behavior was a conflict of interest. Immoral, even."

"Immoral?"

"It was a shitty thing to do."

"Her behavior was shitty. She had a husband and kids."

Still regarding him, Everett tapped his index fingers together. *"You're* sitting in judgment of someone else?"

Drake tried to hide his wince. He was no saint, and everyone knew it.

"She did damn good work for her constituents."

Much better than Bob Finglas was doing in the same position. "The point remains. Someone tipped off the campaign. Right or wrong aside, she should have been more circumspect."

"After what was done to you?"

The barb found its mark, and Drake clenched his fists at his sides. Lorraine's betrayal still stung, even years later. "They're not comparable." Who was he trying to convince? Himself? Or his skilled opponent?

Ignoring Drake, Parker flipped to the next page.

In frustration, Drake dropped into a seat and finished his energy drink. Then, caffeine and God only knew what other chemicals zipping through him, he drummed his fingers on the desktop.

"I'm afraid I'm distracted enough that I've lost my place."

An hour, seven minutes, and three seconds later, Everett picked up the manila folder and straightened the pages. "Everything appears to be in order."

"Good." The thrill of closing a deal humming through his veins, he pulled out a pen from inside his jacket pocket and offered it to Parker.

"You go first."

Yet another power struggle.

Still, he was hungry as hell, and that was enough motivation for him. He drew the packet toward him and signed all the places Smytherson had marked with a yellow sticky arrow.

While he'd been doing that, Parker took a pen of his own from the suit coat still hanging from the back of his chair.

Then, time slowing, the ink scratched the page for the last time.

The deal was done. *Thank fuck.* "We need to get Marcella in here."

Marcella was the photographer many Titans used. Because of her exceptional talent and attention to detail, she was often booked months, if not years, in advance. He and Parker had paid a pretty penny to have her on standby for this evening. But *Scandalicious* would have photos to go with the scoop that would hopefully be the lead article in their morning update.

Before her arrival, Drake checked his hair and fastened the top button on his suit coat. Parker stood and stretched in some crazy ass yogalike ways before turning down his shirt-sleeves and threading the cufflinks back into place. He'd just shrugged into his jacket when Marcella strode in, camera in one hand.

They exchanged perfunctory greetings. After all, Parker's delays had kept her waiting also.

"Let's get some with you shaking hands."

Both had practice at this kind of pose—holding it, and smiles, for an eternity.

After snapping the shutter a dozen times, she glanced up at Parker. "Pretend you're happy about this, Everett. Even if it's just for the picture."

He flashed a quick smile, but it faded damn fast.

"You get that?"

Marcella checked the screen. "Good enough." Then she suggested other shots, including one with the whiskey bottle on the table between them. "Figures. That's the winner there. I'll send you edited photos by midnight." Then she narrowed her gaze. "And a bill for the overtime. I'm late for my next gig."

"Blame Parker."

"I would. Except everyone knows you're a dick." She shrugged before wiggling her fingers and leaving.

The door slammed behind her. Silence hung, dragging into seconds.

"Everyone's a fucking critic." Drake lamented.

"You earned the reputation." Parker shrugged. "Dick." Then he exhaled and grinned.

"I guess we're partners."

"My name's on a deal with the devil."

Drake was a hard callused man who prized winning over everything. Marcella's comment shouldn't have stung. And Parker's shouldn't have landed at all. Yet there they were, chinking the armor he'd cloaked himself in since he'd been a child.

"Might as well drink the whiskey."

Parker hadn't said they should toast or celebrate. His tone dragged with a reluctant resignation. "You pouring?"

"Don't mind at all." Parker shucked his jacket once more. Then he removed the festive red bow from the bottle and cracked open the seal.

Music—like the score to an action-adventure movie—blasted from both of their watches.

Drake looked at Parker who shrugged.

A genius is trying to reach you.

"Bonds?" He scowled. "He rigged the bottle so he'd know when we opened his gift?"

"Typical."

A holographic image of Bonds himself hovered above the watch screens. Drake had heard the devices had that capability, but seeing it was mind-bending.

"Gentlemen! Congratulations are in order."

Was this a recording?

Keeping his left arm steady, Parker used his right to splash some of the alcohol into the waiting glasses. "So you say."

"Tut, tut now. You don't seem entirely pleased, Everett."

So it wasn't a recording. The hologram was a depiction of Bonds in real time.

"Understatement."

"Well, one of us is happy." Bonds smiled. *"And that's all that really matters."*

The man could be an asshole. Was this how others saw him? Shifting, Drake ran a finger beneath his suddenly too-tight collar.

Bonds rubbed his hands together. "We have work to do."

"Fuck off." Drake accepted the glass Everett extended. "It's almost eleven." He hadn't eaten, and he wanted to spend some very pleasurable time with a willing submissive at the Retreat. He'd found very few things more relaxing than swinging a flogger and bringing a woman to exquisite pleasure.

"Slackers. Some of us are still working."

Of course. California was two hours behind Houston. But still, by any measure, it was late. Genius, apparently, never slept. "Go harass someone else."

"Call you in the morning. We'll form a strategy then. I need to buy a couple of politicians."

Parker winced. "That's not exactly what we do."

"Yes, it is." Bonds rubbed his hands together. *"Maybe three*

or four. Oh this will be fun. We'll start with Texas. I want them in my coat before the legislative session starts."

"Pocket."

"What?"

"You want them in your pocket, not your coat."

Bonds flicked a dismissive hand. *"Irreverent."*

This time, Drake didn't bother to correct the misspeak.

"We'll talk in the morning."

Drake and Parker both shook their heads. To Bonds, morning was anything after one a.m.

Then Parker spoke up. "Tomorrow's Saturday."

Bonds frowned. *"And?"*

He had a point. None of them kept regular hours. There was work to be done. And because the deal had taken longer to put together than anyone could have anticipated, they'd wasted plenty of it.

"Cheerio. Tally ho. I'm off."

With a wink and flash of light, Bonds disappeared as if he'd never been there.

Parker picked up his glass. "He could have done a conference call. Video chat, even."

"Bonds? And skip the opportunity to create drama?"

"Excellent point."

Drake lifted his glass in Parker's direction. Surprising him, the other man responded in kind. "To success."

Parker's gaze was intense and steady. "I sure as hell don't fucking plan to fail."

Another thing they agreed on.

But now their success or failure was tied to each other.

He took a drink. "Damn. Even better than I imagined."

"Almost worth the pain of the evening."

"You hungry?" The question surprised even himself.

"You're buying."

Drake shook his head, then drained his glass. "Jackass."

"Better than being called a dick by a gorgeous woman."

Parker never missed a beat. He was a damn fine opponent. After all, he'd come close to getting his candidate elected despite a massive scandal. Still, Drake preferred that they work together.

If either of them survived the experience.

CHAPTER TWO

Three months later

As she dug to the bottom of her purse, searching for keys, Rylee D'Angelo juggled the box of belongings she'd just brought home from her last day at her dream job. Unfortunately it had been a temporary position. And she'd been so good at it that she'd finished the contract weeks ahead of schedule. Her hard work and all the hoping in the world hadn't been able to turn it into a full-time position.

Now the relentless Houston sun, along with its cloying humidity, swamped her, adding more unneeded stress.

Finally she managed to unlock the door to the house she shared with two of her closest friends. Or would until the end of next week when their lease ended.

Rylee used her behind to close the door while she set down her belongings.

Which was nearly an impossible task.

Haphazardly stacked items—lamps and a television, a microwave, and bathroom towels—blocked the path.

Estella, one of her roommates, was getting married soon. Since they all had to vacate the premises anyway, she'd decided to move in with her fiancé earlier than planned. And since she was happy about it, most of her belongings were already in the living room, creating a traffic jam near the front door.

"Hey!" Julianna, Rylee's best friend in the world, popped out of the kitchen, glass of wine in hand.

Rylee admired the tall, athletic woman who'd earned her way through college on a volleyball scholarship. Not only was she amazingly talented, she never seemed to get ruffled by anything. Even starting over on the East Coast.

"You glad to be free of that grind?" Julianna asked.

Rylee'd worked a lot of hours, and she wouldn't miss that part of the job. "Yes and no." She picked up her own box and maneuvered around the obstacle course. Then she placed her belongings on the couch, among all kinds of packing materials.

"Estella's taking the first trips over to her new place in the morning. If you're not careful, she'll take your stuff with her."

"I may not need it anyway." Rylee shrugged. "If I don't find another job soon."

Juliana winced. "You haven't heard back from Francesca?"

Supposedly Francesca was the most amazing corporate recruiter on the planet. She'd found amazing positions for both Estella and Juliana. But so far, Rylee hadn't received any offers. "Not a word."

"Sorry. Just what you don't need…"

"Yeah." Worrying about how she'd pay the rent on her new place by herself, without a paycheck. She was accustomed to sharing in all costs, so this was a big step for her. One she wasn't sure she was ready for.

"Want a glass of wine?"

"Maybe something with caffeine. I'll fall asleep if I stop moving." Since there was no place to sit anyway, she followed Juliana into the kitchen.

"You know what?" Juliana slid her glass on top of the microwave, one of the few empty spots in the entire room. "I think we should forget our problems just for tonight."

"I wish I could." Rylee wanted a bath and to sleep for a week. Unfortunately she needed to apply for as many jobs as she could. Maybe something new had been posted in the time it took to drive home. And her bedroom was only half packed. Going through her book collection would take up a whole day by itself.

She pulled open the refrigerator, and there were few choices. A couple of bottles of water, some Gatorade, half a gallon of milk, and an old pizza box. No soda in sight.

"Estella is going out with her beau tonight. I say we head to the Retreat."

Their favorite BDSM club, located on Buffalo Bayou and not far from their home. Rylee closed the fridge as she grinned. "How did I know you were going to suggest that?"

"You know that's something I really like about you. You're so astute. So perceptive… It's like you're psychic or something."

With a nod, Rylee tapped the side of her head. "That's it. I'm psychic." No matter what the occasion, Juliana suggested a trip to the Retreat. If she was bothered about something, a spanking helped her relax. If she was happy, she wanted to celebrate with a flogging. If she was bored, she wanted the diversion of the hundreds of people who showed up every weekend.

"Who knows? You might find Mr. Right there."

At the outrageous suggestion, Rylee blew out a breath that ruffled her bangs. Maybe that was a possibility—for someone other than her. Less than a year ago, her one attempt at a relationship had crashed and burned around her, humiliating her along the way, leaving her self-esteem in tatters.

It turned out only she believed in forever. And only she thought they were monogamous.

Even if she was interested in another relationship, the Retreat attracted a veritable who's who of Houston elites— football players, newscasters, local celebrities, and more than a few millionaires. A couple of billionaires were rumored to belong. But since almost everyone used a scene name and the club had a non-disclosure policy, discerning information was about impossible.

At any rate, men like those had no interest in her: a struggling young woman who'd worked every day since she was fifteen to pay her own way through life.

"Okay, okay. So maybe not Mr. Right. But how about someone to have fun with? Mr. Right Now?"

She laughed.

"And really, how many opportunities will we have to do this in the future?"

Rylee blinked quickly to banish the tears that rushed into her eyes. After next week, they might never get to go together again.

"I mean, I'll come back and see you."

Turned out Rylee wasn't the only one who was perceptive. "I'm going to miss you."

Melancholy wrapped the room like a shroud. Juliana had gotten a dream job. Unfortunately it was in New York, and for at least the first year, working remotely was not an option.

"Damn it." Juliana sniffled. "Stop getting me all mushy. You'll make my mascara run."

They both attempted brave smiles.

Knowing Juliana would soon be an airplane flight away was another blow in this terrible year.

The realization that their time together was ticking down made the decision easy. "We need dinner first."

Juliana grinned. "Of course."

Rylee shook her head. No doubt that had been her plan all along.

"And don't make us late because you think you look terrible in your sexy stuff." In typical friend fashion, Juliana grabbed hold of Rylee's wrist and tugged her into the bedroom.

As she'd done many times before, Juliana opened the closet door and selected a black A-line skirt. "This is perfect."

"No chance." Rylee shook her head. It ended way too far above her knees.

Evidently not listening, she plucked a tank top off a hanger.

"I'd freeze in that."

"Air-conditioning will make your nipples hard. Doms like that. Makes them want to squeeze them or even better put clamps on them."

"You're impossible."

Juliana grinned. "Another reason you're going to miss me."

"There is no one quite like you."

"Is that good or bad?" Then she shrugged, as the answer didn't matter one way or the other.

What Rylee wouldn't give for a bit of that *fuck-off-if you-don't-like-me* confidence.

"I'll give you one more option." Juliana pulled out a slinky, form-fitting dress that would hug Rylee's every curve.

Wearing it would require more courage than she possessed.

"Ten seconds to make a decision, or I'll choose for you."

Juliana plucked Rylee's duffel bag from a top shelf. "We need this. You can change when you get there."

While Rylee was hemming and hawing, Juliana bent to scoop up a pair of impossibly high heeled sandals. She dumped them into the bag. "Decision made?"

Rylee wrinkled her nose. "I don't like either one of them."

"Ah, but you look like a million dollars when you slip into them. It's like you become a different person. Mysterious even."

"Mysterious?" Rylee scoffed.

"You're the only one who doesn't think so. Now make a decision before I make it for you."

As she studied the choices, both bad in her realistic opinion, she twisted a finger into a tendril of hair. "Uhm…"

"That's it. You're out of time. The tight tank it is."

"No!"

Juliana smiled triumphantly as she tucked the dress into the bag. "That was my choice."

"You're terrible."

"We're going to have a great time."

They usually did. It just took a while for Rylee to commit to going. "I need about an hour to get ready."

"Same."

They studied each other and glanced toward the bathroom down the hall, the one with the luxury shower and oversize vanity.

Game on.

Giggling they both made a run for it. But since Juliana was taller and an athlete, it wasn't a fair competition. But her route had an unexpected box to vault over, and Rylee ended up winning. "First time for everything!"

"Tonight's going to be your lucky night. I just know it."

It took more like an hour and a half to get ready, pull up her hair, apply her makeup, wiggle into jeans, don a loose-fitting shirt, and slip into her most comfortable sandals. Then, after securing her favorite necklace in place, she made her way around the traffic jam of boxes and joined Juliana outside on the front porch.

A few minutes later, their Uber arrived. Thankfully the driver had the air conditioner running on full blast.

Juiliana fanned herself. "In this heat, I was beginning to think I was the Wicked Witch of the North."

"You mean the West. The one who was melting?"

"That's the one."

By the time they arrived at their favorite tapas restaurant, the waitlist was already twenty minutes long. Since the place was so popular, Rylee wasn't surprised. Following their usual routine, they headed for the bar and ordered virgin piña coladas. Since the Retreat had a no-drinking or other mind-altering substances policy, they never had cocktails with dinner.

They dragged their stools closer to each other to make it easier to talk.

"Do you want to see pictures of my new apartment?"

"Yes! You signed the lease?" Sight unseen.

"For a year. Not sure I was ready. But…" Juliana pulled out her phone and opened the listing. "I think our main bathroom is bigger than the kitchen and living room in my place. In fact I'm sure of it."

"But…" Rylee stirred her drink with the thin straw. "It is in New York City. Which, come on, that's spectacular by itself. Think how many people dream of living there."

"Manhattan, baby!" Juliana lifted her glass into the air. "When are you coming to stay?"

"Maybe the first three-day weekend." Flights would be outrageous, no doubt. But having a free place to stay would make up for it. "If I've found a job."

"You will. Francesca will deliver."

Because she wanted to enjoy the evening, Rylee shoved aside her niggling doubts.

"Let's plan on it."

"It's a deal."

"And think about making a trip around Thanksgiving or Christmas. New York at the holidays is an experience you can't miss. Shopping. Ice skating at Rockefeller Center. Shopping. Window displays. Tree lighting. Hot cocoa and a stroll around Central Park."

"And shopping?"

"Did I forget to mention that?" Juliana teased.

They both grinned.

When Rylee's cell phone chimed with a message that their table was ready, they found the hostess. Fortunately they had a booth in the back, which enabled them to talk and to people watch.

The restaurant buzzed with activity, bringing up Rylee's energy level. Maybe going out was the exact thing she needed—well, even if her pocketbook was signaling a dire warning.

They opted to order six small plates and nibble off each.

Then, afterward, they killed some more time at a local ice cream parlor where Rylee ordered a cherry soda with a scoop of ice cream in it. Caffeine and sugar. The very best combination in the world.

A little after nine, they walked over to the Retreat, her nerves stretching tighter with every step. Juliana, by contrast, became more and more animated.

At one time, the building had been a warehouse, then a restaurant. After historic rains from a hurricane flooded the interior, a mysterious LLC had bought the property. It had been rehabbed and restored, but no signs were ever erected. A stunning gloss-black door barred the entrance.

After rapping the heavy brass knocker against the strike

plate, she and Juliana faced a camera. Moments later, the lock released, and they entered.

The foyer was elegant, all polished wood, and church pews for sitting. At first glance, it resembled a historic house.

Taranis, the dungeon master, swept his gaze over them.

Damn. The man unnerved her entirely.

He took a step aside, allowing them to proceed to the check-in desk, staffed by a very competent Miss Watson. If she had a first name, Rylee wasn't aware of it. She wore a tight-fitting gray suit with a black bow tie. She wasn't someone Rylee ever wanted to get on the wrong side of.

Rylee signed the guest register and showed her club ID card before turning over her cell phone. It was one way to ensure no one snuck any pictures.

"Welcome, Anne."

Being referred to by her scene name always threw her off. But she appreciated the fact the club took great pains to protect privacy. "Thank you, ma'am."

She nodded sharply, then used two fingers to call Juliana over.

Next, they headed to the table where a colorful array of wristbands were laid out. The evening's hostess smiled at them. "I know a lot of Fridays are Ladies' Nights. But tonight's an exception."

Rylee and Juliana exchanged glances. Juliana shrugged.

"It's Gentleman's Delight. Which means that our gentlemen, or people identifying that way, have a little more leeway than usual."

Juliana leaned forward. "Tell us more."

"If you're available to scene, you can select a yellow bracelet. Blue is for 'leave me the fuck alone.'" She laughed. "And of course, you're always free to decline any invitation. Club safe word is *red.* You never need a reason or excuse."

Each visit, they were reminded of that inviolable rule.

Juliana reached for yellow.

After a deep breath, Rylee followed suit. Not that anyone would ask her to scene, but just in case…

They each rolled the colorful elastic in place, then opened the wooden door that led into the club's cavernous main area.

Instantly her senses spun into a sense of overwhelm.

EDM music thumped out a loud rhythm, accelerating her pulse. Anticipation, maybe? Or fear? She wasn't sure, but there was no doubt adrenaline, maybe cortisol, hummed through her.

The club's reported manager, someone she'd only seen once, the mysterious Altair—referred to as Your Grace by ordinary members of the Retreat—had spared no expense in making the Retreat a special place to visit. Though the club operated under low protocol rules, there was a level of decorum. And all the equipment was high-end, most of it hand-hewn by a renowned Colorado Dominant. Projector screens streamed video from other parts of the club.

Though there were maybe a hundred pieces of equipment, they were spread far apart, allowing a lot of space for participants to wield their toys of choice, including single-tailed whips. Interested spectators had plenty of viewing space as well.

The Retreat also had numerous rooms lining two of the building's exterior walls—medical examination rooms, a full-on jail cell, a cupping table, and even a meditation/tantra area.

A vendor fair occurred every weekend, and this was no exception. Each night, a huge spread of food was set up on a banquet table. A world-class coffee shop occupied one corner, but the main attraction was the bar. The imposing piece had been imported from Arizona, and Wyatt Earp had supposedly taken a drink while standing in front of the massive, ornate piece of art. Since no alcohol was served at the club, the scarred wooden relic with its wavy mirror behind it now served as a great place to meet friends or enjoy the parade of interesting people passing by.

She and Juliana headed for the ladies' room to change into their club attire.

When Rylee exited her dressing room, she stood there to admire her friend. Juliana was breathtaking in a halter top that left her midriff bare. Her skirt ended just below her buttocks. She'd donned platform shoes that made her legs even longer.

"It's no wonder Doms fight each other off for the honor of spending time with you."

Juliana shook her head. "Girl, it's both of us!"

Rylee wrinkled her nose and tugged down on the hem of her dress.

"Stop that!"

The attempt had been futile anyway. The material slid right back up to where it wanted to be.

"You look magnificent. Own it."

She'd kill for an ounce of Juliana's confidence.

"Your eyes are smoky."

"It's part of my mysterious allure." She attempted to keep a straight face, but she ended up laughing.

"Well it's working. Let's go find some men whose only desire is to make our wildest fantasies come true."

"Lofty goals." Nothing like that had ever happened to Rylee.

Near the entrance, they each stowed their bags in cubbies designed for that purpose.

"Where do you want to start? The bar?"

"Sounds good." That would give them a chance to see who was in attendance.

"Through or around the perimeter?"

A sudden sense of boldness surged in her. "Through."

This evening, for the amusement of Dominants, several Jacob's ladders had been hung from the industrial overhead beams. For safety, crash mats lined the polished floor. No doubt some evil Tops would demand their bottoms be wearing very little while they struggled for control and stability as they attempted to ring the bell dangling from the top.

They managed to find two stools at the end of the bar. And because the mirror was massive, they had a good view of what was happening on the floor behind them.

A broad chested man with long pink hair flowing over his shoulders appeared in front of them and placed coasters on the wood. "What can I get you?"

Juliana didn't even glance at the menu filled with non-alcoholic delights. "Mineral water with lime, please."

"You got it." Then he looked at Rylee.

She drummed her fingers. "Diet soda." The caffeine might keep her up all night. Or maybe not. The entire week, she hadn't gotten enough sleep.

"So…" Juliana leaned in closer. "There are two guys back there…" She moved her head to the right.

"And…" She followed Juliana's gaze.

"Have a look."

Rylee's already accelerated heart rate rocketed through the roof. "Damn." They weren't *guys*. They were full-on gorgeous, stunning men. Gentlemen, even.

And intimidating as hell.

Both were over six–feet tall, athletically lean, and dressed in tailored clothing—they definitely stood out from the rest of the club crowd. The one on the right ,with dark blond hair brushed back rakishly, wore a white dress shirt, tantalizingly unbuttoned at the throat.

And the man on the left...? Exhaling, she rubbed her arms to soothe away the sudden goose bumps.

He appeared lethal.

His dark hair was a little long, sleek. His slacks and jacket were black, and he'd opted to complete the look with a matching shirt. And even from a great distance across a dark space, his eyes radiated laserlike intensity.

The two turned toward each other as if in conversation, breaking a spell she'd somehow fallen under.

"What do you notice?"

Rylee shook her head. How long had Juliana been speaking? "What do you mean?"

"They've been checking you out."

"Me?" Her voice was a loud squeak. "No. No, no, no. Nope. Maybe you. They are absolutely, positively not looking at me." They would have no reason to. Men like them could have any woman they chose. In fact, no doubt they fell all over each other to capture their attention.

The bartender delivered their drinks. "Anything else, ladies?"

One of the nicer things about the Retreat was the yearly membership fee covered most beverages and all food.

"We're good. Thank you." Juliana squeezed her lime into her glass. "And I'm serious. They've been looking at you."

"And your imagination is running away with you." But when she hazarded a glance back at the mirror, they were still standing where they had been.

Was it her imagination, or did the blond gentleman's gaze connect with hers? Regardless she was captivated. As she continued to look, he slid his hands into his pockets.

A Dom who often played with Juliana approached them, arrowing purposefully toward his bottom of choice.

"May I join you?"

Juliana grinned and flashed her wristband, signaling she was available to scene.

"It's my lucky night," the Dom said. "I've been wanting to paddle a beautiful bottom, and yours is amazing."

"Why thank you, kind Sir." Juliana grinned.

She'd accepted the compliment in a way Rylee wished she was capable of.

Before sliding off her seat, she looked at Rylee. "Will you be okay if I leave you?"

She nodded. "Of course." It wasn't unusual for them to split up after they arrived at the club. Generally they checked on each other throughout the evening. Most times they shared a ride home when they were done playing. But every once in a while, Juliana went home with someone she was playing with. And occasionally she wanted to go out for a meal with others after playing. Rylee, on the other hand, wanted a bath and her bed, which was one of the reasons they called an Uber on club nights. They were each free to make their own plans. And one of the dungeon monitors always made certain that ladies leaving alone were escorted to their vehicles or the rides.

When Juliana hesitated, Rylee reassured her. "I'm fine. Go have fun."

"You deserve to have a great evening." After winking, Juliana slid from her stool and fell in step behind her temporary Dominant.

Alone, Rylee sipped her drink through a straw.

But she couldn't resist another peek in the mirror.

The men were walking toward the bar. Probably to take a couple of empty seats at the far end.

But they didn't change directions.

And then... They closed in on her. There was no doubting their intention.

As if by prior arrangement, they moved in next to her,

standing at the end of the bar.

The dark haired one on the left scared the hell out of her. He reminded her of a panther, sleek and graceful and slightly terrifying. Very real feminine intuition screamed a warning to flee far and fast while she still could.

The other gentleman—if either could be called that—had a gentler presence, or at least less threatening. His gray eyes held kindness. Then he blinked, and it was replaced by a cool, calculating gleam. Had she only imagined the earlier emotion? Had it been there at all? Maybe a trick of the light? Or just her fanciful imagination?

Then the man on the left spoke again. "We've been watching you."

God, his voice was hypnotic. As deep as it was rich.

He leaned in just a little closer. His eyes captivated her. Almost amber and predatory. She tried to look away but was helpless, trapped within his compelling gaze.

"I see your necklace."

Without thinking, she touched it.

"Is it a collar?"

She shook her head.

"So you're not under a Dominant's protection."

"No…" Rylee struggled with how to finish her sentence. Instinct urged her to address him formally, but protocol didn't demand it. Right now, despite his overwhelming and Dominant air, she had no connection to him. And thirty seconds from now, he'd likely turn on the heel of his very expensive shoes and walk away.

"How remiss."

"I'm sorry?"

"If you were mine, I'd have you collared, and you'd never be left unattended for anyone to approach."

The world spun, and her breath seemed to freeze some-where in her diaphragm. *If she were his…?* The idea was absurd. Something out of a fantastical fairytale. For someone else who wasn't her.

"And you're here to scene." He inclined his head, indicating her wristband.

Where was this conversation going? Were they toying with her? The blond didn't seem like the type, but the other... She wondered if he had a cruel side.

"We haven't met."

The blond had spoken, shattering the building tension. Relieved, she directed her attention toward him. Anything to escape the gravitational pull of his friend.

"Everett Parker." He extended his hand.

His voice was soothing, like a cool evening rain, and his grip was reassuring. "Uhm...Anne." Had she really stumbled over her scene name? Absently she wondered if his name was also made up. It suited him.

"My pleasure...Anne."

"Ours." The other man cut into the conversation. *"Our* pleasure."

Courtesy dictating that she also greet him, she gave him her full attention, something he seemed to command as well as demand.

"Drake." He was bolder than his friend. Instead of the politeness she expected, he lifted her hand and kissed the back of it intimately, in a way that had her wayward heart galloping toward fairytales and happily ever after. No man had ever treated her that way.

She wasn't sure any man had ever done anything like that to her before.

"Is this your first visit?" Everett seemed to be the one with the greatest social skills.

Rylee couldn't help but smile.

"Was that funny?"

"Sorry. Just reminds me of the pickup line. 'Do you come

here often?'"

Everett grinned. "I'll give you that. It was a pickup line of sorts. And not as smooth as I hoped evidently."

His honesty disarmed her, and she responded in kind. "I come here every once in a while with my friend." Rylee wasn't sure if she would have the courage to attend by herself.

"And you have been known to enjoy a scene?"

"It's amazing stress relief."

"And has it been a tough day?"

Day? Thirty of them—in a row. "Year." Rylee wasn't sure where the admission came from. Maybe because this whole situation was surreal. She might not ever come back now that Juliana was venturing into her new life. Which meant she'd never run into this pair of dangerous, charming men again.

Drake, obviously over the easy chitchat, changed the direction of the conversation. "Have you ever played with two guys before?"

To cover her shock, she took a drink of her soda. "No." Most times she didn't play with anyone. But the idea secretly thrilled her every bit as much as it terrified her.

"Anne, I'd like to thoroughly Dominate you while Parker here plays with you and paddles your ass."

She froze.

Everett winced. "What my Neanderthal friend means is—"

"I said what I mean, Parker."

Did he always refer to his friend by his last name?

Then Drake leaned forward, smelling of masculine determination. He fingered her necklace then placed his finger alongside her carotid artery where her pulse fluttered like a butterfly. "I want to thoroughly Dominate you and ruin you for any other man."

CHAPTER THREE

Rylee resisted the impulse to pinch herself. If this were a dream, she suddenly—maybe stupidly—didn't want to wake up.

Still, a nagging, incredulous part of her refused to be silenced. She vowed not to be any man's plaything ever again. Last year, she'd believed Peter had loved her. His awful comments to her when she found out otherwise nearly destroyed her soul. *"You're the kind of woman men fuck, not marry."*

She needed to be sure this wasn't a horrible game to them. "You can't mean this."

"On the contrary. I've never been more serious in my life."

"Why me?"

Everett responded. "Are you kidding me? You're beautiful."

With a small laugh, she shook her head. She'd believed that kind of smooth-talking lie once. Never again. "Even if I believed that, there's no shortage of gorgeous women here tonight." Most who wouldn't hesitate for one second to agree to what either of these men suggested.

Drake didn't seem to have the same patience as his friend. "Do you see me—us—looking at anyone other than you?" He leaned in just a fraction of an inch closer, and his presence overwhelmed her. "You were watching in the mirror."

So much for her clandestine skills.

"Deny it."

She remained silent.

"You know we were watching you."

Juliana had said as much, even while Rylee had remained oblivious.

Everett shot Drake a quelling glare, not that it seemed to have any impact. "We'd enjoy—very much—spending some time pleasing you."

For another few moments, she debated. The night could be amazing if she kept her heart on a short leash. Playing with them didn't have to mean anything. But still they needed boundaries. "It's just for tonight."

"For a start." Drake's counter was immediate, as if he'd anticipated her response.

Before Peter, she'd have never been capable of what she said next. "Then I'm afraid I'll have to decline. Thank you for your interest."

"Thank you for your interest?" Drake snarled.

Everett, however, smiled. "The lady is making a simple request."

"She's being insulting." Though he responded to his friend, Drake didn't take his gaze off her.

Was he feral? Rylee shivered. Drake, whoever he was in real life, was definitely not the kind of man to cross. Wondering who this new, bold version of herself was, she responded in kind. "If you're offended, you're welcome to go find someone else to scene with." *Hell's bells.* Her voice shook with emotion she was trying to hide.

"I know what I want." He continued to invade her space.

Numerous dungeon monitors—obvious from their navy T-shirts with DM in great big gold letters—were spread throughout the club, watching every interaction. Security cameras were prevalent as well. It would take less than two seconds to get rid of Drake and Everett.

"But if the scene goes as well as I intend, then I'd like the opportunity for us to pursue this further."

That he dulled the sharp claws he'd flashed at her meant something, and she exhaled.

"Drake would simply like the opportunity to see you again if you're agreeable."

"I can fucking speak for myself."

"Perhaps." Everett shrugged. "But not well."

Once again, the less unnerving man made her smile.

"Give us a chance?"

Drake looked at his companion. "Asshole."

Everett's grin was quick and easy. "Dick."

Were they always like this? Partners or foes?

"What do you say, Anne? Will you forgive Drake's lack of tact and agree to give us a couple of hours of your time?"

Hours? She'd never had a scene that lasted more than twenty or thirty minutes. But maybe Everett was optimistic.

"We promise you won't regret it."

His tone reassured her enough to once again give into her inner bold woman that she hadn't met before tonight. "The answer to your question is no. This is for tonight only."

Drake scowled. "I reject your ultimatum."

Her heart fell. "In that case, I have to wish you a good evening."

"What he means is we accept." Everett spoke for both of them.

She hazarded a glance at Drake.

A dangerous pulse ticking in his throat, he bowed. "We're honored to play with you."

"Do you have toys of your own?" Everett, as always, soothed the situation, asking the question before she had the chance to second guess herself. "No."

"I have a toy bag."

At Drake's announcement, she shivered a little, wondering what implements he preferred, and more, what kind of Dominant he would be.

Then Everett spoke. "Typically I like to use my bare hands on a submissive."

Unable to help herself, Rylee looked at his massive hands and wildly imagined him spanking her, teasing her.

"But tonight I suggest we visit the vendor fair. I'd like you to select something that appeals to you. A souvenir that you can take home with you to remember the evening."

His solicitous personality appealed to her more than Drake's abrasive one. So why was she equally attracted to both?

"A paddle, maybe?"

Desire rippled through her. That was one of her favorites.

"But before we go any further, both of us need to know your limits."

Until right now, she'd always been the one to bring up that conversation, something the Retreat made easy. The club had very specific requirements before joining. Prospective members had to attend a series of classes. The first was held in the private room of a local restaurant. It was meant to feel relaxing. Vanilla clothing, something she would wear on an ordinary day, was the rule. Subsequent gatherings were held at the club itself, during nonplay hours.

Taranis, the dungeon master, had led the first discussion. *"After all, we need to feel comfortable if we're going to get naked together."* Not that she'd ever taken off many of her clothes.

Dominants and submissives were on hand to discuss almost everything club related and to offer demonstrations.

Every time the group met, two things were reinforced: the Retreat's safe word and how to negotiate a scene. Role play was essential so that bottoms had the language as well as the confidence to say what they needed to for themselves physically as well as mentally and emotionally.

By the time she arrived for her first actual visit—something very different, under dim lights with thumping music and Tops who were willing to spank her ass—she was armed with every possible tool to enjoy herself.

But now she wondered if she would have remembered to bring up limits if Everett hadn't. *Would Drake have asked?*

Aware that the two were waiting for her response, she nervously toyed with her straw. "Don't leave me alone."

Drake ensnared her gaze. "That didn't need to be said. I protect the woman I'm with. My submissive."

She swallowed deeply. "And, uh, small bruises are okay, but nothing more." Except for the piercing pagoda and tattoo parlor reportedly on the second floor—a place she'd never seen—nothing that might mar the skin was permitted in the building.

"How sensitive is your skin?"

Of course, the concerned question came from Everett. Again she marveled at how different the two were. "Not very."

"Good." Drake's tone rang with pleasure and authority. "You'll have something to remember me."

Fear entwined with desire and began to snake through her. In the most shocking way possible, his words aroused her.

Everett sighed. "How about a slow word? And anything other than *red* for stop?"

She followed the easy guidelines Taranis had suggested. "I like to keep it simple. *Yellow* and *red*."

"Anything we need to know?"

Rylee shifted. "I'm not all that experienced."

"Never had a permanent Dominant?" Drake never seemed to settle for the superficial.

"No."

Voice soft, uncompromising, he corrected her. "You mean *No, Sir.*"

God above. That powerful elixir of fear and desire hammered her again.

"Say it."

"No, Sir." The words, the respect, flowed easily as if her world had fallen into its natural order for the first time. "I never had one." She paused. "Never desired one." *Until this very moment when she wanted two.*

"If you run into issues, you'll say so?"

Grateful to Everett, she severed the unholy connection with Drake. "Yes. Yes, Sir."

He offered her a cheeky grin. "I prefer Everett."

"Yes… Everett."

Shaking his head, he placed a hand on his heart. "The way your tongue wraps around those syllables…"

If she had met him when he was alone, she might never have wrapped their evening in an ultimatum. But they came as a pair. And she could not imagine Drake tolerating her playing with Everett and leaving him out.

"Shall we?" Everett offered his hand to help her down from her stool.

"Thank you."

Drake was drumming his fingers on his thighs in an impatient staccato as he waited for her to comply.

Then she was standing between them, and their massiveness overwhelmed her. From the perch of her chair, she'd only had to tip her head back a tiny bit to meet their gazes. But now, even in her tallest platform heels, she didn't even come up to their chins.

"Tiny thing."

Heaven help her, Everett was sweet. *Tiny?* She'd been called short or even petite, but never that, not with her curves.

She started to pull her hand away from Everett's grip, but he simply tucked her arm into the crook of his elbow.

"Tonight you're spoken for. We want others to recognize that."

Drake growled. "Yes. *We* do."

"You should try being a gentleman instead of a caveman." Everett's recommendation was light, earning him a snarl that he ignored.

Instinctively she tightened her buttocks. Everett might be comfortable needling his companion, but it was her body that Drake would soon be marking.

On the way to the booths, they passed the Jacob's ladders where two half-naked bottoms were struggling to maintain balance. One of them had his rear prominently sticking up in the air and was being urged on by his Top's flogger.

Attempting something like that was her worst nightmare.

"Don't worry."

Had Everett read her mind? Or maybe she'd communicated that with the way her body had tightened.

"We're not going to push you to do anything outside your comfort zone."

From her other side, Drake added an addendum. "Within reason."

Even though she glanced around, she didn't catch sight of Juliana.

The vendors were doing some business, but not huge amounts.

"Anything appeal to you?"

She eased her arm from Everett's. The prices on the items

were outrageous, way more than she'd ever spend. "Uhm... You can just use your hands. I don't need any of these things."

A small smile toyed around Everett's mouth as he looked at Drake, and something unspoken passed between them.

"Or maybe borrow from Drake?"

"I don't share." Not surprising her, he was implacable. Then he looked at her. "With certain exceptions."

"Choose something." Everett redirected her attention. "Paddle, perhaps?"

They spent a few minutes looking at items, and she returned again and again to a purple leather paddle.

"What do you like about it?"

"It's my favorite color."

He picked it up and smacked it several times against his palm. "It's good. Thuddy, maybe a little stingy." He looked at the seller. "May I?"

"Of course, Sir."

"Please place your hands on the table in front of you, Anne."

Her mouth fell open. "Here?" She gulped. "Now?"

"Did you need me to repeat myself?"

Had she been wrong about him? Earlier he'd seemed nicer. She'd even flirted with the idea he might have been showing tenderness. "No."

Trembling, she did what he asked.

"Look at me."

Unable to resist Drake's soft command, she did as he said.

"Keep your gaze on me." He placed a reassuring hand on top of hers.

The juxtaposition between the two men's behavior was a total mindfuck. Who was who?

Leaving her dress in place, Everett rubbed her rear.

Pins and needles of desire rocked her world.

His touch was firm and sure. He knew exactly how to arouse her.

Then he released her and laid the paddle against the underside of her buttocks and gave several gentle test strokes. "Ready?"

Still captivated by Drake, she nodded.

"Please answer him." He stroked his thumb across her wrist.

"Yes, Everett."

He spanked her hard, enough to feel it through her clothes but not enough to frighten her.

Right away he soothed away the small pain. Maybe it was her imagination, but it vanished.

"How was it?" It was a congenial inquiry. They could have been talking about the weather.

She closed her eyes to search for the honesty he expected. Revealing herself wasn't easy. "Pleasant."

"That's a rather weak response."

"I mean...I liked it."

"Harder, perhaps?"

When she opened her eyes again, Drake was still in place, regarding her. "Yes, Everett." Was she really asking for the gorgeous Dominant to spank her again, right here in the vendor area?

Neither he nor Drake seemed at all perturbed.

Everett swung again, this time with more force, and she lifted her heels from the floor. She slowly let out a breath. More than she'd been willing to admit, she'd needed to come here tonight.

"Better?" This time the question came from Drake.

"Yes, Sir."

"Wasn't as bad as you feared?"

In fact, the illicitness had given her a shot of excitement.

Everett smoothed her dress. "I think this will do." Everett

offered the implement back to the woman. "We'll take it. No need to wrap it up. Just cut off the price tag."

"Of course."

"You may stand up." Drake lifted his hand.

Until he'd spoken, Rylee hadn't realized she was still in place. In mere moments, the pair had managed to help her get lost inside her head.

Everett pulled out his wallet and turned over a credit card.

"Spreader bar?" Drake asked Everett.

"Not a bad idea."

Now Drake perused the offerings, picking up an adjustable metal bar with cuffs on the ends.

It appeared wicked, and even more so when he weighed in in his palm. "Sturdy." He offered it to Everett who nodded in agreement.

Was Drake contemplating purchasing it?

"I'll take it."

Seriously? She'd seen similar items online for a fraction of the cost. "Sir, that's—"

"Is it on your limits list?"

She hesitated. "No. But—"

"Then we will certainly enjoy using it with you." He leaned toward her so no one else could overhear. "And as you'll find out, I'm selfish. I think you'll like the fact I keep your legs apart, leaving you throbbing and vulnerable to my touch."

She grabbed the table to prevent the world from spinning.

"So I'm going to keep the bar. But it's yours. Anytime you wish to repeat this night, all you have to do is find me."

That was not happening. *Never.*

He grinned as if they shared a secret. "It's my intention to please you in all kinds of wicked ways."

And it was hers to keep herself from falling for them.

Once Everett had accepted his paddle, Drake nodded to the seller to confirm his purchase. "Put it on Altair's account."

Rylee cocked her head to one side. Just who was this man, anyway? She'd only seen the owner once and in passing. He had a commanding presence that demanded respect from everyone he encountered.

That Drake referred to the man casually and said to charge the purchase to his account left her reeling.

"Of course."

The woman grabbed her electronic device and asked him to use his fingertip to authorize the purchase. "His Grace only allows certain people to do that."

"He owes me a few favors."

In a handful of seconds, the transaction was complete.

This time, before Everett had a chance, Drake stood beside her and placed the palm of his free hand flat against the small of her back. Everett acknowledged the move with a half shrug.

Without a word, Drake guided her to the cubbies to collect his black leather bag, then took her hand and led her deeper into the main dungeon.

Each moment drew them closer to the inevitable, and her knees wobbled in response.

Drake found an empty space toward the back corner, which offered them a little privacy—something she was grateful for. Both men placed their purchases on a nearby chair.

The space had an O-ring that was attached to a pulley descending from a steel beam. Everett crossed to the wall to lower it, cocking his head to one side to ascertain Rylee's height. Which left her standing in front of Drake, wondering what to say or do, while coaching herself not to give in to the urge to change her mind.

But if she allowed the cloying fear to overtake her, she'd never know if the experience was as magical as she hoped it would be.

"I'd like you to take off your dress."

She'd been afraid he'd say that. Having Everett spank her through the garment had helped preserve her modesty as well as her dread of being found lacking.

Waiting, he folded his arms across his chest.

"You can trust us." Everett whispered his promise into her ear.

Drake nodded his agreement. "Believe him."

She nodded. If they were disappointed in her curviness and showed it, the evening would end. Right now, with the furious butterflies beating inside her, that would be okay. In fact it might be preferable. She'd have the rest of her life to get over the hurt. "I'll be keeping on my bra and panties." At least she'd dressed in matching, somewhat sexy under-garments.

The men exchanged glances.

Rylee understood some clubs had stricter rules than others. The Retreat allowed women to be topless with their nipples uncovered. Thongs were requested in all public areas, however. But she'd never bought anything skimpier than bikini bottoms.

"If that makes you comfortable." Everett spoke for both, though the narrowing of Drake's eyes informed her he didn't necessarily agree. At least he didn't offer an argument.

They remained where they were as she scooped her dress up and off. With her eyes closed, she dropped the garment.

One of them sucked in a breath.

"As beautiful as I imagined."

That was Drake. She'd know that growly voice no matter the distance.

When one of them captured her chin and tipped it back slightly. She had no choice but to respond to the unspoken command.

Drake.

Approval was written in the hard amber depths of his eyes. "You're luscious."

"I…"

Everett grinned. "Thank your Dominant for his approval."

No one had demanded that of her before. She wasn't good at accepting compliments, and this one was more difficult than others. Maybe because his opinion mattered, and it shouldn't. Her emotions were messy, complicated things. "Thank you, Sir."

For the first time, Drake smiled. The radical act transformed his face, making him more inviting.

"When you're ready, I'd love to see your entire body, naked and spread wide, on display for us."

Her mouth was so dry she couldn't respond. *Not in this lifetime.*

"Everett has a home with a well-equipped dungeon of his own. We'd be happy to host you there anytime."

"I'm comfortable here."

Everett grinned. "She just told you to fuck off."

"The offer remains."

Did he know how to accept *no* as an answer? Was she the only woman, submissive, who was able to resist him?

Not that it was easy. No matter how terrifying she found him, his aura of confidence tempted her to ignore all her internal alarm bells.

"Miss Watson will have my contact information with permission granted to share it with you. Just call her and ask."

"I'll keep that in mind." When he scowled at her polite rejection, she attempted to dull its edges by adding his requested honorific. "Sir."

With a sharp nod, he left, saying he was in search of a wheeled caddy.

"Is he always this intense?" she asked Everett when they were alone.

"Ignore him." Everett shrugged. "Winning is his love language." He paused. "Maybe his only language."

Moments later Drake returned with the cart, and he thumped his bag onto the top shelf. And in the light, she noticed an owl emblazoned on the side. Unusual. And she had no doubt it had some meaning.

Her heart picked up more beats as he shrugged out of his jacket, then plucked out cufflinks that he tossed into the bag. As he did so, bright green, the color of emeralds, flashed in the light.

Gaze on her, he purposefully turned back his shirtsleeves.

Everett did the same.

Drake loosened his tie, then unknotted it. Instead of leaving the ends to dangle down his chest, he continued pulling on the silk. "I'm going to tie your arms behind your back while I get organized."

"For no other reason than it pleases him." Everett shrugged.

"Yes, Sir."

"I don't mind if you're a little uncomfortable."

Everett reassured her. "It's not meant to hurt you."

"Yet." Drake's response was instantaneous.

The sooner they had her secured to the overhead ring, the better. If he uttered more promises like that, she wasn't certain she could remain in place.

Tie in hand, he moved behind her, and Everett took a step in her direction to cup her shoulders.

She crossed her wrists behind her.

Everett pushed her shoulders back a little. "That's it. Stick out your gorgeous breasts."

Drake secured her wrists, then tugged his bond even tighter.

He checked to ensure it wouldn't cut off circulation, but it was tighter than she expected, ensuring the posture he intended.

"May not have been a good idea." Everett tucked a strand of her hair back. "You look so hot it's difficult to focus."

Had he read a book about how to impress women?

Drake walked around to the front of her. "I have to agree."

As he continued to remove belongings from his bag—whips of every type and a couple of things she didn't recognize—she tracked his every move, mesmerized.

"Do you enjoy nipple stimulation?"

She shook her head to concentrate on what Everett had asked. "A certain amount. Yes."

"You've worn clamps before?"

"Lightweight ones."

When Drake was finished, he stood in front of her. "Are you averse to us giving you an orgasm?"

The question left her speechless.

"I'm taking a guess that you've never had one before while playing here?"

Once again, Everett's astuteness was impressive. "Is it that obvious?"

"I think it's time you found out how that can make a scene extraordinary."

More than once, she'd gone home at the end of night, still turned on. And she'd mentally replay events as she used her vibrator. "I'm open to it."

"It *will* happen." Drake's words were confident.

She tried to roll her shoulders in nervousness, but his knot was sure.

"Are you ready to begin?"

"Yes, Sir."

Everett untied her. "Go ahead and put your hands over your head."

Once she had, he cuffed her and attached her wrists to the O-ring, then left her to adjust the pulley so that she was stretched taut, but not enough to force her onto her toes.

Then Drake picked up the spreader bar. He fastened one ankle into place while Everett worked on the second.

The pair worked in harmony. No doubt this was something they did all the time. Which set off warning bells in her head. To her, this was an incredible, one-time experience that would rock her world. To them, it was another fun night out, a casual diversion that meant nothing. Forgetting that might devastate her.

"You really are beautiful, Anne."

Everett's words echoed with earnestness, and his gaze held no lies. She wished she could believe him.

Drake trailed a finger around the shell of her ear, then lower, ending when he reached the bow on the front of her bra.

Her breath was frozen. Even if she weren't tied and with her legs apart, she wasn't sure she'd be able to move.

Drake lifted his finger, leaving her skin both on fire and chilled at the same time. He reached for a small flogger, then held it in front of her. *Purple.* He'd listened.

"Do you prefer to start with a flogger? Or with the paddle?"

"I... I don't know."

Everett moved behind her and began to rub her buttocks through the delicate material of her panties. "So very spankable."

She preferred that to *abundant.*

He rubbed her shoulders, her back, and her upper arms. Though she battled nerves, his touch soothed her.

"We'll start with the flogger."

Naturally Drake would make the decision for her.

Her Dominants switched positions, and Drake placed the broad leather strands on her shoulder, then drew them back in a slow, sensual dance. Then he repeated his action across her other shoulder.

Moments later, the falls all but caressed her buttocks, then her back as he wielded the implement with measured strokes.

She'd never experienced anything this rhythmic—one side of her body, then the other in turn, as if he were creating some design on her body.

Through her bra, Everett cupped her breasts. They ached for him. She opened her mouth to communicate that, but no words emerged. The Retreat's staff had spent hours coaching her on how to communicate the things she didn't like or wouldn't tolerate. But Peter's betrayal had shattered her confidence, leaving her unable to ask for what she *did* want.

"More?"

"Yes, Everett." *Yes. Please.*

Thank God he didn't make her beg.

The flogging continued, and Everett squeezed her breasts, pushing them together and up.

She was lost in the overwhelming duality of being fondled while Drake rained leather kisses all over her backside.

"Is this pleasing you?"

Rylee thought that was Everett's voice, but somewhere along the way, she had stopped paying attention and instead, surrendered.

"Anne?"

SIERRA CARTWRIGHT

She murmured a sound that she hoped passed as an answer.

"I'd like to play with your nipples."

They ached already. "Yes."

Everett slid his fingers inside her bra cup and teased one nipple to a full, hard nib. As much as she could, she arched her body toward him.

He responded to her wordless request, capturing her other nipple and giving it equal, exquisite attention.

This experience was stunning. She'd given herself over to a Dom on a spanking bench, been attached to a St. Andrew's cross, and already these wildly handsome men had taken her places she'd never been.

Without her being aware of it, Everett released her and took a step back. Suddenly Drake and his flogger, its strands starting to bite, were everywhere, her buttocks, thighs, the fronts of her legs, her sides, and midriff.

Lost, she allowed her head to tip to one side.

On and on it went. Rylee whimpered but from the exquisite push-pull of pain vanquished by immediate pleasure.

"Look at me."

She'd been lost inside herself, and Drake's rough voice dragged her back to the present. He stood in front of her, filling her vision, making her heart race.

"I want you to realize you've turned yourself over to me."

Yes. His words made her wild with need. "Yes, Sir."

His hands were on her, and he squeezed her nipples hard, making her tremble as arousal cascaded through her.

Then a pain, different from the previous one, lanced her buttocks. It occurred to her that Everett was using the paddle, placing some of his spanks over marks that Drake's flogger had left behind.

She wasn't sure she'd ever been more turned on.

"Are you ready for that orgasm?"

"Please." She hadn't believed she could get there, yet she was already on the edge, desperate for the desire burning in her to be quenched.

Behind her, Everett tugged on her panties, wedging them between her legs, abrading her clit. She cried out. But they weren't done with her. Drake moved a hand over her pussy. He cupped her, holding her mound possessively as if he owned her.

"Look at me."

She'd be lost if she did.

"Anne." Not one to be denied, he captured her chin. *"Look at me."*

He'd gone from predator to conqueror. She was captured, and she was his.

"You see it. You know it."

But she couldn't admit it.

The paddling continued, stinging, forcing her body forward, and always Drake was there teasing her through the damp scrap of material.

A reckless part of her wished she was brave enough to ask him to slide inside her. He had her on a cliff-edge of emotion. And she hated that he knew that.

"I'll prove it." Like Everett had earlier, he slipped a hand inside her bra and rolled her nipple between his thumb and forefinger.

It was as if he knew all the right things to drive her toward climax.

"That's it. Come for us." He teased her clit with just the right amount of pressure. "Give me what you've got. Come in my hand."

Powerless to resist their ruthless determination, she trembled, and then she screamed as she found her satisfaction.

But he was relentless. "I want more."

His words about ruining her for any other man drifted through her sensual haze.

"Keep looking at me. See how much I love pleasing you."

Shockingly she shattered a second time.

"That's it. All of it, Anne. Everything you've got, I want."

Crying, she sagged against him, straining the bonds.

He wrapped his arms around her, soothing her as Everett released the O-ring, so that her body was more comfortable.

When her breathing finally returned to normal, Drake stroked her hair. "You're exquisite."

The softer side of Drake—now that he'd won—was even more impossible to resist.

"You're made for this. For us."

Frantically Rylee shook her head. She had to keep her mind straight. She was no longer capable of settling for being a rich man's play toy.

While Everett took exquisite care to rub the circulation back into her arms, Drake crouched to release her ankles. His face was inches from her, and she was assailed by the tempting urge to hold his head and draw him closer.

Scandalized by the thought, she sucked a breath.

She wasn't this bold, brave woman she'd pretended to be.

In the morning, she'd wake up back in her regular life, while they found another submissive to play with.

She had to get out now before she was sucked into their vortex.

"Are you okay?" Everett asked, standing next to Drake.

Was she? Maybe. Unharmed. But changed.

"How was it?"

Were there words? Maybe, but not in her vocabulary. She had to settle for something that didn't come close. "Amazing. Thank you both." How was she supposed to do this? Pretend it had been ordinary and hide behind polite conversation.

Every scene she'd had before this had been easy. But these two had undone her. She really had given Drake everything she had.

Everett picked up her dress and helped her into it.

With a quick smile, she smoothed the front, as if her actions could hide her emotions like they did her body. "This was enjoyable." Her voice wavered as if ready to fracture. "Thank you both."

He tucked a strand of hair behind her ear. "I'm looking forward to learning even more about you. Your responses. The things that excite you. What are your most secret desires? Wildest fantasies? The things that drive you. Your needs. We want to know every one of them. I promise you this: I won't stop until you've revealed everything."

So he could use them against her? She'd learned that lesson. She'd trusted Peter, and he'd thrown her deepest emotional secrets in her face. Drake and Everett weren't just asking for her to scene with them again, they were asking for a piece of her soul. "I need to go."

"Anne…"

She shook her head.

Drake captured her wrist, and she yanked it free, making her escape bravely, without ever looking back.

CHAPTER FOUR

"What the fuck?" Frustrated and not understanding what the hell had gone wrong, Drake plowed his hands into his hair and took a step to follow her.

"Don't."

Parker's voice cut through Drake's delirium and the raw hunger to have her.

"I mean it."

He snarled at his partner. Just because they occasionally hung out at the Retreat and played with the same woman, it didn't mean they were fast friends. Closer than they had been months ago, but there were miles between them. The rift—finding trust—might take years.

Anne moved as quickly as the throngs of people and her tight dress and heels allowed her to. She didn't slow down.

And she didn't look back.

Curse it to hell.

With every step she took away from him—from them—something inside him died.

How long had it been since he felt this kind of attraction? Months? Years? He couldn't let her go.

Then she vanished from view. "She must be grabbing her purse. Or looking for her friend. Maybe she needs a ride." If she left alone, her safety was at stake.

"Let her go, Drake. Trying to stop her is against club rules."

The rules could piss off.

He started toward the exit.

Parker grabbed Drake's arm and got in his face, nose to nose. "Back down, Drake."

Agitation gnawing on his self-control, Drake scowled at Parker. "So what the hell is wrong with you that you can let her walk away?"

"I'm not the fucking enemy, remember?"

"You're going to tell me that the scene wasn't spectacular? Something special? Or that I imagined her reaction?" She'd cried out as she'd climaxed against his hand. He could still feel her warmth.

"I was here. I experienced it as well."

"And you're still willing to let her go?" He snapped his fingers. "Like that? As if it didn't mean anything?"

"I don't like it any more than you do."

"So how can you be so damn nonchalant?"

"Is that what you think?" Parker shook his head. "You couldn't be more wrong. We all shared a powerful attraction."

That was part of it, no doubt. With her long dark hair and divinely feminine curves that begged for his attention, she was exactly the type of woman who appealed to him. But it went beyond that, into a realm he'd never been to before. Her brown eyes were laced with distrust, but it warred with desire.

She might have visited the Retreat before, but she was more innocent than experienced. As he'd noted earlier, she needed the protection of a Dominant. Of him.

Parker released his grip and not a moment too soon.

Drake was about to succumb to the urge to deck the man. That would be a satisfying outcome right now.

"We need to be reasonable. All ladies are escorted to their vehicles or rides."

Didn't matter. They'd scened. Seeing to her safety was his job.

Parker continued to talk in a calm, measured way, the tempo no doubt honed over the years he'd dealt with difficult candidates. "Taranis was watching the end of the scene, and he's not the only one."

No doubt Parker was right. The dungeon was getting progressively more crowded, and they had no doubt attracted at least a small crowd.

"Taranis is still keeping his eye on you."

"And?"

"If you don't control your impulses, you're taking a hell of a risk. There are cameras. Lots of them. And you may be friends with Altair, but there's no way he'll let you keep your membership if you violate his rules. He'll have no choice but to have you escorted out."

He hated that Parker was the voice of reason. And that added fire to Drake's fury.

"Look. Go home. Have a drink. Workout. Regroup. Formulate a new plan." Parker cracked a grin. "Or as you call it 'a winning strategy.' We can come back tomorrow, next weekend, and the one after that to look for her. But that's not going to be possible if your membership is revoked."

He exhaled. Parker's calculating dose of logic finally got through to him, enabling Drake to harness his impatience if only for a few minutes.

Finally Taranis turned his back and strode toward a different part of the club. Via his earphone and mic, he was in touch with all the dungeon monitors and Altair.

If anyone believed Drake would leave things as they were, settling for defeat, they were mistaken.

Parker's watch chimed with an incoming message. "Look, I have a meeting at the Braes with a potential new client. You're welcome to join us."

"I'll pass."

For a few seconds, Parker hesitated. "Don't do anything rash."

Still looking toward the exit, hoping for a glimpse of her, Drake didn't respond.

Parker picked up his paddle. "Still need to give this to her."

"I'll deal with it."

"Fuck off." The words might be light, but they were deadly serious. "I'll handle it myself. See you in the morning?"

"Yeah."

Minutes after Everett clapped him on the back and left, a couple asked if he was almost done with the space.

"Yeah." Altair was expecting him, and Drake was suddenly looking forward to the meeting. If anyone could help him with his mystery sub, it was the owner himself.

He repacked his bag, then wiped down the O-ring and the caddy. As he was leaving, an object on the floor shimmered in the overhead lighting, capturing his attention.

He crouched to pick it up. Anne's necklace. Earlier the small heart had been pristine. Now the metal was marred a little. "Well, well." After a slight hesitation, he closed his hand around the memento and slid it into his pocket.

Drake took his time wending his way through the club. Despite Everett's words to the wise, and aware of dungeon monitors still watching him, he strolled the aisles looking for Anne's friend.

He never saw her.

His thin hold on his temper began to fray again. He didn't like to be thwarted.

After stowing his gear in the cubby once again, he returned to the lobby to collect his phone. He sent Altair a message. Not that the man didn't already know that Drake was on his way.

He gave Miss Watson a curt nod. "Buzz me through?"

"Certainly, Sir."

He strode toward the side wall, then stepped around some artfully arranged potted plants before pushing on a wooden panel. The craftsmanship was exquisite, which meant no one would notice it was a door rather than part of the wall.

Beyond that was an elevator controlled by biometric access.

Drake stood in front of the scanner, then pressed his finger to the call button.

Instantly the doors parted, and he was whisked to the second floor of the building. He exited into a wide-open space that Altair Montgomery shared with only certain people. The man valued his privacy. From what Drake knew, no one had ever been invited to the third level where he lived.

"Welcome." Altair was waiting, a drink in hand for Drake.

Appeared to be whiskey. No matter what was in the crystal glass, he needed it. "Bonds?"

"Is there anything else?"

"Thank you." He accepted the glass and followed his business associate into the half of the floor that served as a gathering place, and it could easily accommodate fifty people without feeling cramped. There were numerous couches and chairs, a bar, and a full kitchen. This evening, a massive projection screen hanging from an overhead wooden beam showed camera feeds from all over the club.

The remainder of Altair's massive area was behind rein-forced concrete walls, much like a bank vault. Drake didn't know much about Altair's business or its need for secrecy. He was rumored to be in business with Bonds and working on AI and augmented reality—something he thought was more important to the future than the much-lauded virtual reality.

"Join me."

Altair had angled two chairs toward each other, a small table between them.

Once Drake was seated, Altair grinned, then spoke. "It appears you enjoyed your evening."

Fucking voyeur.

"The young lady in question left something behind."

The gold was nestled in his pocket. "I'll keep it safe."

"Miss Watson can see to its return."

"I said I'll keep it safe." Before taking a sip, Drake lifted his drink in acknowledgment of Altair. Damn, it was good. "Bonds knows his spirits."

"He does indeed."

Though Drake wanted information about Anne, he harnessed his impatience and bided his time. Altair had requested this meeting.

"I'm interested in land in Austin."

After a second sip, he put down his glass and sat back to listen. "Go on."

He'd met Altair through Bonds. Though neither of the men were inclined to invite him into their business dealings, Altair used various corporations for his property acqui-sitions.

"Silicon Hills."

The nickname for the area where a lot of high-tech busi-nesses were located on the west side of Austin, Texas's state capitol. "I thought you'd never move there."

"I am not. Hate landlocked places."

He made no secret of the fact he loved to take his sailboat out onto the Gulf of Mexico, and Houston provided easy access for the recluse.

Plenty of people were satisfied sailing on some of the impressive lakes in the Austin area, but Altair was not one of them. The bigger the challenge, the more he liked it.

Altair smiled and set down his drink—that appeared to be untouched. "Bonds wants a place out here. Favorable tax situations."

Part of the work he and Parker had been doing on the Genius's behalf.

"Lots of jobs."

"I'm confused. Bonds's team would be able to negotiate a great deal from the city if he builds there."

"I want adjoining land."

Now he understood. Infrastructure to support the new campus. And that would be pricey.

"Interested?"

"In what way?" Was Altair hoping Drake would invest? Or merely examine contracts?

"I'd like to continue the arrangement we have here."

There were several other partners in the deal, and it was only for this building. Altair paid a considerable amount of money to rent all the floors, so the risk was minimal.

But the Austin deal would require substantially more money.

"First round of ten per investor. Twelve of us."

He resisted the impulse to reach for his glass. *Ten million dollars*, to get started. And it could be years before they saw any ROI. "How many in so far?"

"Five. I'm closing the offer in a few months. Give everyone time to conduct due diligence."

"How many rounds of funding?"

Altair propped an ankle on his opposite knee. "As many as it takes."

So he could be looking at fifty million, even a hundred. He could do it. But did he want to? Funds he tied up here weren't available to use other places.

"Do your analysis. Talk to your accountant and advisers. Bonds sends his regards."

Code for Bonds wanted him in?

"Send me what you've got?"

"It'll be in your secure email by the time you arrive home." He leaned forward to pick up his drink.

They chatted for a few more minutes, with Altair promising to show Drake one of his augmented reality scenarios on his next visit.

"Imagine this. Your submissive has a secret desire to have you fuck her in front of a dozen people. And you don't care for the idea. In my simulation, you can be alone, at your house, but we can give you an audience. Each person will appear to be viewing, or having a side conversation, perhaps enjoying their beverage of choice. It's not virtual because you won't be required to wear a device or special suit. No touchpads."

He was intrigued.

"Sounds, scents."

"Is there a purpose?"

"One of the most basic of our three human needs."

Altair often went on a riff about his beliefs. For survival of the species, humans needed three things, a healthy fear, and access to food. The third followed suit. "Fucking."

"The money will follow."

Drake hoped he wasn't as jaded. Until tonight, he feared he was. "Back to your original scenario."

Altair rolled his still-untouched glass between his palms.

"I need to know about her." When Altair didn't respond, he clarified. "Anne."

"Hmm."

Man was fucking stoic. "What do you know about her?"

"I protect my guests' privacy."

Drake exhaled his frustration. "Damn it."

"The night is young. There are plenty of other submissives here. And many would leap at the opportunity to scene with you."

To Drake, it didn't matter if there were a thousand willing submissives lined up in front of him. None would have the appeal of the brown-eyed, long-haired beauty who had no idea of her allure and sexiness. "You're implying submissives are interchangeable?"

"Are they not?"

For the first time since his ex, the formidable Lorraine James, had cut him to the quick, he didn't notice any other woman. He was single-mindedly focused on Anne. The first order of business was to uncover her real name. After that, he'd find out who'd hurt her. And he'd make whoever it was regret every action. "Not this time."

Altair nodded. "I see."

No doubt he did.

Drake wasn't without resources, and he intended to find her even if he had to knock on every door in Houston.

After finishing his drink, he stood. "She made it to her car safely?"

"We see to all our guests' needs."

"That's a yes?"

Though Altair nodded, he didn't speak. "That's all the information I'm prepared to divulge."

"In that case, good night."

Altair didn't stand to walk him to the elevator.

He stalked to his car and once inside turned over the engine to turn on the air conditioner.

Despite the hour, he placed a call he knew would be answered.

"Drake." Celeste Fallon sounded neither tired nor stressed. "To what do I owe this call?"

Another reason he appreciated her. She wasted zero time on idle chitchat. If it wasn't important, he would have reached out during normal business hours.

She owned Fallon and Associates, ostensibly a PR firm. And maybe at times the company did provide that service. But their specialty was crisis management. For more than a hundred fifty years, they'd specialized in high-profile cases, restoring reputations, saving careers, ensuring people didn't open their mouths. Her resources were vast, spanning the globe. "I need to find someone."

"I'm listening."

He pulled out her necklace and dropped it in the console. As he outlined the evening's events, he traced the outline of the heart. He gave Celeste most of the details. After all, she'd no doubt heard everything in her years of operation.

"And after this magical evening…she ran away."

Didn't sound so magical when Celeste repeated his words back to him. "I think she was nervous. Maybe a little scared."

"Of you, Drake? Difficult to imagine."

He thrummed his fingers on the dashboard. "I want you to find her. I'll pay whatever it costs."

"No."

Stunned, he froze. "No?"

"Clubs have very strict rules. Your submissive chose to keep her identity secret. I respect that. And so should you."

Should. Couldn't. "After she left, I found her necklace."

Celese gently laughed. "Like Cinderella."

"What?"

"You know, the fairytale."

"I'm not familiar." His childhood wasn't normal, and he had huge gaps where others didn't.

"To make it short…Cinderella was poor. And she had the opportunity to attend a ball where Prince Charming was going to choose a wife."

How the hell did this relate to his life?

"At any rate, Cinderella and the prince had a lovely evening. But at midnight she ran away. Her carriage would turn into a pumpkin, you see."

"No, I don't see."

"When she fled, she lost one of her glass slippers. The prince knocked on every house in the kingdom until he found the woman whose foot fit the shoe."

"If that's what it takes. I'll use every fucking resource."

"I'll tell you this, Drake. You are no Prince Charming."

❧

Close to ten p.m., and somewhere in her new apartment, the faint sound of Rylee's phone ringing caught her attention.

Juliana, maybe?

Grateful for the interruption, despite her exhaustion and the fact her bath was already running, she used her hip to close the kitchen drawer she'd been putting silverware in and went in search of the device.

Her bedroom, maybe?

She navigated around the boxes that sat in silent judgment, waiting for her to finish assembling her bookcases—something that it turned out was more difficult than she anticipated. Surely there were some missing screws or something.

The phone fell silent.

Realizing the water was close to flooding over the bathtub rim, she quickly shut it off.

Would she ever get settled?

Or accustomed to being alone?

For four years, she'd had roommates, always someone to talk to, hang out with, flip through television shows with until something caught their attention, hotly debate what was for dinner and whose turn it was to pay.

Now, despite the fact she played her music, the rooms echoed with loneliness. There were no mad dashes to the best shower, she didn't have to wash anyone else's dishes, and no sneaked treats from her secret chocolate stash. And she'd never been more miserable.

And it seemed as if she'd been that way since her evening at the Retreat. Juliana had enjoyed herself, but Rylee wished she hadn't gone.

Being the focus of Drake and Everett's attention had rocked her world.

Drake had skillfully and easily made her climax, and they'd shared a connection that had been missing in her life.

But she was smart enough to realize she meant nothing to them.

Things would be better if—when—she found a job that paid enough to cover her rent.

Next week, she intended to take a part-time job at her local restaurant as a server, something she hadn't done since her first year of college.

The phone rang again, and she hurried to find it.

Somehow it had found its way beneath her bed.

She snatched it up and glanced at the screen. *Francesca.* The corporate recruiter. *Finally.*

Rylee took a deep breath to steady her thumping heart. Francesca had to have good news. Right? After all, why call at nearly ten o'clock otherwise?

Despite her attempts to remain calm, her hand was shaking, and it took two swipes to answer the summons.

"Rylee? Francesca here. I've got something for you."

In silent gratitude, she closed her eyes.

"It's an executive admin position at a law firm. Here's the deal. Right now, it's a temp position. Six months is what the owners are looking at."

Not again. "Any chance of it becoming permanent?"

"Yes. For the right candidate." She named an hourly wage that made Rylee blink. "At the three-month mark, you'll receive a five-thousand-dollar bonus. Ten thousand more at the end of the term."

This was almost too good to be true. She could not only pay her car note and her rent, but she'd be able to make some progress on her student loan debt. But instead of leaping at the chance, she hesitated. "Why is the position available?"

"There are only two partners so far, but the office is very fast-paced, and they will be growing. They want someone with the flexibility to help take them to the next level." It was the recruiter's turn to be a little quiet as if choosing her words carefully. "It's been a bit more challenging than our last placements expected."

Reading between the lines, she gathered it was a stressful environment.

"You've worked in a downtown law firm before, if your resume is correct."

"Yes."

"So it shouldn't be anything unusual or difficult for you."

While she wanted those bonuses, they were being offered for a reason. "What are the hours?"

"Eight to five-ish. Maybe longer if required on occasion."

"Is there an employment contract?"

"The usual. I'll send it over."

Helping a business grow sounded exciting, but the bosses

sounded as if they'd be a challenge. And from what Francesca said, they were having difficulty keeping her position filled. Drawing a breath, Rylee took the biggest gamble of her life. "In that case, I'd like double the salary."

"Done."

The reply had come so fast that Rylee wished she had had held out for more.

"We need you to start in the morning."

In a few hours? She shook her head. "On a Friday?"

"Is that a problem?"

"Not if there's a signing bonus available."

Francesca hesitated, and Rylee wondered if she'd pushed too hard.

Then finally Francesca replied. "I can do one week's salary."

That resolved, Francesca outlined further details. "As part of your responsibilities, the owners require that you pick up coffee every morning."

She'd done that before, but not for a couple of years when she'd taken her first position as a junior admin.

"You'll be given an account at the coffee shop in the building. And they don't mind if you order yourself something."

At least that was something considering she wouldn't get nearly enough sleep tonight.

"And be sure the refrigerator is stocked with energy drinks."

What the heck kind of office was this?

"I'll text you the address, and I'll send over the employment agreement. Just get that back to me first thing."

A dozen questions crowded her brain.

"Be there no later than eight. You'll find a detailed list of responsibilities on your desk. I think that's it." She paused for a fraction of a second. "Good luck, Rylee."

Before she had a chance to sort through her thoughts and ask another dozen questions, Francesca was gone.

She considered giving Juliana a quick update, but since it was an hour later in New York, opted not to. Besides, she'd have more details after she finished her first shift.

Simultaneously relieved and anxious, Rylee undressed and sank into her bathtub. But aware of everything that still had to be done, she couldn't relax. Instead she hurried.

Wrapped in her robe, she sat in front of the computer that sat on the kitchen table.

Not surprisingly, Francesca had already sent through everything Rylee needed to handle, including tax withholding information, and her employment agreement which she quickly read and then signed electronically.

After handling that, she entered the address of her new job into her GPS app. Fortunately the law firm was in a downtown high-rise, not more than twenty minutes from her place. But still, she had no idea where to park or how long the coffee order would take.

Then she googled the company, K and G and Associates, so she had some idea of what to expect.

Surprising her, there was little information to be found, and no website was listed. What kind of growing firm that could afford to pay her an outrageous wage didn't even have a landing page?

Unless she was willing to turn over her credit card number to pay for a deep search, something she was skeptical about, the only results available were the address and a phone number. Intrigued, she dialed. Since it was after-hours, she expected voicemail, which was exactly what happened.

The female voice on the recording was polite but unrevealing, inviting her to leave a message that would be returned the next business day. No options to press one for a certain person or department.

Strange.

But they'd been vetted by Francesca, and she had found great jobs for her friends.

Telling herself she'd find out soon enough, she headed for bed. But once she got there, she tossed and turned, unable to fall asleep.

As usual, she slept badly and hit the snooze button. Twice. Which left her running late. And all that was made worse because she wasn't exactly sure where she was going or where to park.

Still blurry eyed, she somehow managed to make it out the door by seven. She only had to walk a few blocks, but the parking lot had been more expensive than she'd anticipated. And the line at the coffee shop was ridiculously long. If she was expected to do this every day, she'd need to discuss her work hours with her bosses. It would add at least fifteen minutes to each day, and frankly she'd rather sleep in. Maybe she could leave before five and beat some of the traffic?

When it was her turn, the barista greeted her warmly. He was wearing a nametag that read Kevin and was framed in stickers of stars and the sun. She appreciated his cheery smile.

"You're new."

She grimaced. "First day on the job. And I'm supposed to pick up coffees for my bosses."

"The lawyers?" When she nodded, he pulled out two large cups and scribbled on them with a bright orange marker. "I gotcha covered."

She didn't know him, and already she liked him.

"And for you?"

"Something large." She hadn't had time for more than one

cup of coffee, and she usually needed three to fully function. "Frothy. Sweet."

"Caramel or chocolate?"

She eyed the donuts in the case to her left. "Caramel."

"Extra shot of espresso?"

"Why not?" She had no idea when lunch was coming, and she needed something to sustain her for at least four hours.

While Kevin whipped up her drinks, she studied the other offerings. In addition to the pastry case with treats and sandwiches, he had a separate refrigerated case stocked with salads and protein plates, along with chilled beverages.

When her order was complete, he pressed the cups into a tray to make them easier to carry.

"I see you eyeing that donut." He grabbed a piece of tissue paper.

With a grin, she nodded. "I'll take it."

He rang up the order and asked her to initial the receipt.

"That's it?"

"Except for my daily reminder. Make good choices today."

She exhaled. "I'll remember that. Thank you."

As she moved away, he greeted the next customer. "Morning, sunshine!"

So far the day wasn't off to a bad start. But then the elevator was crowded, she turned the wrong way on the third floor, had to backtrack, and found suite 312 at four minutes after eight.

Pasting an apologetic smile on her face in order to make a good first impression, she juggled her tote bag and the tray as she turned the knob and opened the door and froze on the spot.

In her college career, she'd worked in numerous professional offices, and she'd never seen anything like this.

The reception area had a desk piled with papers and all

sorts of other stuff, including unopened boxes, a stack of mail, old coffee cups. At least a hundred paperclips were strewn across the surface.

When had the last person quit? Had she walked off the job? Not that Rylee blamed the other, unknown person.

After closing the door, she ventured deeper into the office.

There were three doors that she could see. Two were closed. One, a little farther down a hallway, stood open.

Deciding that was the best place to begin her exploration, she headed that direction. As expected, it was a conference room. And the table was equally as disastrous as her desk. Still, she moved a ream of copy paper out of the way to set down her tray.

She pulled her cup out, took a fortifying sip, then noticed the refrigerator. Remembering what Francesca had said, Rylee pulled it open and found an empty box of energy drinks as well as a shelf fully stocked with bottled water.

Francesca had been adamant about the job responsibilities. Caffeine and caffeine were the first two priorities. Making a mental note to order some, she continued through the suite, finding a copy/mailroom that was totally unorganized with its trashcan overflowing, a workout space—that was unexpected—and a bathroom with a shower—also unexpected. Though she'd worked at places where she knew senior executives had their own private washroom, she'd never seen one that was for all employees.

Francesca had noted that the partners wanted to grow. But where would they put another person?

Her first order of business was caffeine, likely followed by a day of organizing. After weeks of having her life unsettled, packing and unpacking boxes, that was the last thing she wanted to do, especially in a pair of heels and a skirt that was borderline too tight.

She returned to the main area, and since both doors were still closed, she returned to the lobby to buy most of Kevin's stash of energy drinks.

Carrying the weighty bag, she rode the elevator back upstairs. This time, it wasn't as crowded. Maybe the lull between the people who started at eight and the more fortunate who didn't have to report until nine?

With her practiced smile in place once again and expecting the disaster that would meet her, she opened the door, only to freeze in place.

Drake—the man who'd haunted her every dream for the last few weeks—was perched on the edge of her desk, arms folded across his chest. He was grinning triumphantly, and his cup of coffee was right next to him.

The bag fell from her nerveless fingers, and cans clattered as they smacked, then rolled across the hardwood floor.

No. No, no, no, no, no. This couldn't be happening. Coming face-to-face with him in real life was her worst nightmare.

And right now, she was frozen in place, riveted by the deadly gleam in his haunting, hunter-like eyes.

"Well, well. We meet again…Anne."

CHAPTER FIVE

"I ...uhm..." She trailed off to draw a deep steadying breath. What the hell was she supposed to say? How was she supposed to act? Initial shock slowly receded, unfreezing her muscles and replacing it with an urgent need to flee. "There's been a mistake. I must be in the wrong place. If you'll excuse me...?" Why was she asking permission?

"Suite 312." He lifted one shoulder. Confidently. Arrogantly.

Frantically she shook her head. Was it her imagination, or did he not look surprised to see her?

"I promise, you're in exactly the right place."

Before their scene ended at the Retreat, his voice had been harsh with demand. Now it was a little gentler with a reassuring note beneath it. Still, she didn't have the courage to continue this conversation, especially before nine o'clock and without her coffee. She pivoted to grab the doorknob

"Welcome to K and G and Associates. We're glad to have you aboard."

He continued speaking in his unruffled manner as if she wasn't on her way out.

SIERRA CARTWRIGHT

"I'd like you to hear me out."

She shouldn't.

"Please."

Rylee was powerless to resist the softer side of him.

With a soft sigh, she released her grip and turned back to face him. But she pressed her back to the door, keeping the distance of the room between them. "You know I can't work here."

"Oh?"

"Are you dense?"

His lips quirked. "That's a new one."

She winced, wishing she could take back the question. She hadn't meant for it to fall out of her mouth.

But that didn't change the fact he'd seen her nearly naked. His flogger had caressed her body, hands had been inside her bra, and he'd held her pussy and given her an amazing orgasm.

She'd submitted to him, and he'd thoroughly and completely owned her. Never, even with Peter, had she been so vulnerable. And she couldn't afford to open herself up to any man like that ever again. When—if—she ever dated again, it would be with a man who was...uncomplicated. Someone who was down to earth, someone she could connect with. Rylee was done with rich guys who acted like they could have anything and anyone they wanted, consequences, like her feelings, be damned. "I'll let Francesca know this isn't a good fit."

"Actually we think it's perfect. We've been looking for good help, and your resume was quite notable."

She narrowed her eyes. His words were making it sound as if he hadn't known she was the woman he and Everett had scened with.

"We're willing to give you a try. Even though it cost us a pretty penny."

76

"You offered the salary."

"Not exactly."

Furiously, intrigued though she didn't want to be, Rylee scowled. "What do you mean?"

"Francesca told us what we had to offer to get a candidate of your quality."

Estella had insisted that Francesca negotiated hard on behalf of her clients. Maybe she had worked her magic on Rylee's behalf. And if she walked away without even trying, would she land another position this lucrative?

"And then she offered you bonuses."

Had she not been authorized to do that?

"Including one for signing." He nodded toward the cluttered desk. "Your check is right there."

This wasn't fair. That money meant a lot to her—the difference between comfort and continual struggle—and would be difficult to walk away from.

"You also have a sense of integrity, if my guess is correct." He'd remained where he was, unthreatening, behaving in a calm, appealing way that she didn't associate with him.

"I thought perhaps your signature on your employment contract, committing to a six-month agreement, might mean something to you."

"You don't play fair."

"No, Rylee. I don't."

Suddenly Everett's words from the night they met returned to haunt her: *"Winning is his love language. Maybe his only language."*

Had she ever faced a more difficult decision?

The phone on her desk rang, and he nodded toward it. "You're being paid handsomely to answer it."

"It may not have occurred to you that I haven't had any training.

"I'm sure you'll do fine."

A fight warred inside her, one between her sense of responsibility and need for self-preservation. Ignoring a business call wasn't something she was comfortable with, despite her feelings toward the company's owner.

"Impress me."

Damn him. She brought her chin up. And his challenge was one she immediately rose to. At this moment she despised her sense of competitiveness.

"That's two rings. On the fifth, it goes to the auto attendant. Obviously something we try to avoid."

"You could answer it yourself."

"I could. But I'm paying you to do so."

That had nothing to do with it, and they both knew it. His behavior was a power play, nothing more.

With a sigh, she pushed away from the door and stepped over the cans of energy drinks as she hurried to the desk.

Rylee took the long way to the desk, keeping as much distance between her and Drake as possible. The man seemed to have a tractor beam around him, and she had to stay far away from it.

The phone trilled again, as she reached for the handset, she noticed her check—her name in big, bold letters—sitting next to it.

Meeting his gaze, she exhaled.

She had moments remaining to answer the phone. Fortunately there was a script taped to the desk to make it easier. She silently blessed the former employee who'd had that foresight as she doubted it had been Drake. "K and G and Associates. This is Rylee. How may I help you?"

A woman with a clipped, no-nonsense voice demanded to be put through to Mr. Griffin.

"You'd like to speak to Mr. Griffin?" Rylee repeated, looking at Drake for guidance. She had no idea who that was.

He pointed to himself and mouthed the words. *"That's me."*

The first time she'd heard his full name. Drake Griffin. Harsh syllables to fit a lethal man.

"Who is it?"

"May I ask who's calling?"

The woman huffed. "Lorraine James."

"One moment, Ms. James. Let me see if he's available."

He made a cutting motion across the front of his throat. Struggling to suppress a smile, she turned her back to him. "I'm sorry Ms. James. I'm afraid he's not available. May I take a message?"

"Send me to voicemail."

"I'm afraid I'm new here, and I am not quite sure how to do that."

"Shit." The woman exhaled her extreme annoyance. "They can't keep anyone working for them. Assholes."

"I'm sorry, Ms. James." Why was she enjoying this? "Was that the message?"

"Jesus. Is this your first job as well? No. Tell him my client is willing to meet at three p.m. His office. And tell him not to be fucking late this time."

"Of course, Ms. James." She met Drake's gaze. *"Don't be fucking late."*

He grinned.

"Is there anything else I can—" Rylee winced as the phone was slammed down on the other end of the line. "Wow." With her ear still ringing, she met Drake's eyes. "I assume you caught that."

"Every word."

"She's a…" She trailed off. Badmouthing others wasn't necessarily a good way to move forward. For all she knew, the two were friends.

"World-class bitch?"

"Uhm…"

"And my former girlfriend."

Unable to formulate a response, she opened and then closed her mouth. "I'm not sure what to say." *Good thing she's your ex?*

"Your competence is impressive."

His opinion shouldn't matter. But it did, elating her.

"Great job in handling her. She didn't stress you out?"

"It takes much more than…"

"A world-class bitch," he repeated.

"What you said." Rylee shrugged. "To ruffle my feathers." It took a spectacular man to unnerve her.

"You're going to be a good fit here. That's your number one responsibility. Being a gatekeeper."

"I thought it was keeper of the coffee and energy drinks."

"Speaking of… I see the energy drinks." That were still strewn about the reception area.

"The coffee, cold by now, is on the conference room table."

"So far, Rylee, you're batting a hundred. I'll have to let Francesca know she did well."

She frowned, refusing to capitulate. "I still haven't agreed to work here."

"Ah. Well. We only want people who want to be here, part of an exciting growth opportunity."

Was that what he called it? "It looks more like a total disaster."

He raked back a hank of hair. "There you go again with that brutal honesty."

And there he went again, being so sexy that she couldn't help but respond on a heated, feminine level. "I showed myself around earlier. You have a disorganized mess. It's not a surprise that people keep quitting."

"We're building new offices. Doesn't seem to be much point in getting settled here."

"I disagree."

"Respectfully?"

"Not at all." She smiled. The word Sir was on the tip of her tongue, but she refused to spill it. "I have opinions."

"So I'm learning."

"As I said, I can tell Francesca I'm not a good fit."

"I disagree. Disrespectfully, also."

She scowled.

"We need someone on the team who can help us grow, keep us on track. We're not just looking for an admin. We're looking for an executive."

Her eyes widened.

"That's why this position was only listed at six months. It's our intention that you—if you're the right fit—hire the staff you need."

Trust him to arrow her words back at her. "So you're saying that if I'm wonderful, I get to be your office manager?"

"No. A team leader. Someone who sits in on the owner-ship meetings and provides input."

Oh God. It was her dream job. Why did it have to come from him?

Protectively she wrapped her arms around her middle "Drake…" Is that what she should call him? "Mr. Griffin—"

"Drake is fine."

Maybe for him it was, but keeping a professional distance between them by addressing him more formally would be smarter.

"Do you have a hard time envisioning where you want to go, and how you want your life to turn out?"

At one time, she'd been more of a dreamer. Life—and Peter—had shown her otherwise. "I am more of a realist."

"Humor me."

No way would she reveal any more of her heart to him. "You're paying me a good salary, and honestly you probably don't need much more than an admin. I mean, the office is small…"

Mirth played around his eyes. "Go on."

"Two people. You don't have a website. No social media pages. It's like you barely exist, and it will take years for you to build the sort of practice you're talking about. The city is filled with much larger firms that have been in business for generations." She knew. She'd worked in two of those offices. One of them spanned two floors in a pricey building. "From what I've seen, you're not all that busy. One phone call since I've been here." The company she'd worked for during her sophomore year in college had partners that worked almost nonstop and dozens of admins who worked until at least eleven.

"I see."

The other office door opened, and Everett emerged.

Stunned, she shook her head as if he were an apparition.

When he finally noticed her, standing behind the reception desk, he stopped in his tracks. "What the actual hell?"

It appeared only one partner had been expecting her.

He shot Drake a quelling glance. A quick peek in his direction showed he was completely unconcerned.

Drake merely adjusted his tie. "Say hello to Rylee D'Angelo, our new executive admin."

"Are you out of your ever-loving motherfucking mind?"

Seemed she and Everett were in agreement once more.

"A fortunate coincidence. I called Francesca. And this morning, Rylee walked through the door.

"A *fortunate coincidence?*"

Seemed Everett didn't believe Drake any more than she did.

"You and I need to talk."

"Her resume is in your inbox. Experience vetted. College degree. Perfect fit."

"We're going to talk." Everett shook his head as if to clear it. Then he looked at Rylee. "I'm unsure what to say."

Drake dropped his hand into his trouser pocket. "Maybe welcome aboard. Instead of being an asshole."

Good grief. What was it between these two?

"Anyone want their coffee?"

She and Everett responded at the same time. *"Yes."*

Drake headed to the conference room, leaving her alone with Everett.

"Rylee? That's your real name?"

She nodded.

"I apologize for Drake."

"It could be a coincidence."

"Yeah." He glanced over his shoulder.

"Winning is his love language. Maybe his only language."

"Are you okay?"

She nodded. "Trying to decide what to do."

"I mean since that night." He shrugged. "As well as now."

"Yes. Just fine." Her smile was bright and as fake as the plant in the corner as she hoped to convey that it hadn't been one of the most significant experiences of her life.

He glanced around the office. "What the hell happened here?"

"I arrived with coffee. Since both of your doors were closed, I showed myself around. I saw the energy drinks were low on stock, so I went back to the lobby to buy some." She wrinkled her nose. "When I returned, Mr. Griffin was sitting on my desk. To say the least, I was taken by surprise."

"I'm sure that was one of you."

Drake returned, tray in one hand, her donut—with a bite missing out of it—in the other.

She scowled ferociously.

Noticing, Everett spoke up. "You don't eat pastries."

"Oh. Was that yours, Rylee?"

"My breakfast." And damn it, she'd already earned it.

"My apologies." He offered it to her.

Putting her mouth where Drake's had been? "Keep it."

With a shrug, he took another bite.

"Dick." There was some force behind Everett's observation. But when he addressed Rylee, he was much more solicitous. "I'll go downstairs and buy you another one."

"I'm not hungry anymore."

Drake picked up one of the cups. After scanning the writing on it, he offered it to Everett. Then he read the second. "Caramel?"

"Not yours," she said, reaching for it.

He took a drink of his before perching on the edge of her desk. "I'm glad you joined us, Everett. Rylee was informing me that she sees a lot of room for growth, and that it will take some time."

His interpretation was a gross mischaracterization, but she didn't correct him. It wouldn't matter if she didn't join the team. She glanced at Everett who was still regarding her with utter kindness in his eyes. If the company were just owned by him...

She banished that thought. It wasn't. And even if it were, working for a Dom she'd played with would be worse than a bad idea.

"And she did some research on the firm last night."

Two minutes on Google, but yeah...

"And found nothing." The dick took another bite of her donut. "She didn't have our names, however."

She glanced from him to Everett. What was she missing?

"The firm might be new, but we're not. The lovely lady you spoke to earlier? My ex...?"

"Lorraine called?" Everett raised his eyebrows.

Drake smiled. "He who speaks first loses."

The more she knew him, the worse he was. Did he treat everything in his life as a zero-sum game? And why? What the hell drove a person to behave that way?

"She and her client will be here at three."

Everett whistled.

"You're invited to sit in, Rylee."

"I won't be here."

"Ah. As I said before, we only want people who want to be on the team."

She took a sip of her drink, wishing it was hotter, but at least it was satisfying her hunger cravings.

"Tell her who you are, Parker."

"It's more who I was." Everett shrugged. "Someone whose candidate lost a recent election."

Rylee glanced at him.

Drake named the senator, and Rylee gasped, glancing at Everett. "You worked on her campaign?"

"Don't let him be humble. He managed her first run and her second."

"I thought she was going to win."

"She probably would have." Everett shrugged. "But the opponent had some help." He leveled his gaze at Drake. "We'd worked together before. He knew how I operated, how we'd do damage control. He was a step ahead the whole way."

No wonder the animosity could be thick. How were they friends at all?

Apparently unperturbed, Drake didn't respond. "Everett is known as the Oracle."

She didn't follow politics much, but she'd heard of him.

"*Was.*"

"The Kingmaker."

"Working on regaining my crown."

"You never lost it. One loss doesn't erase three dozen wins."

Rylee tried. She tried. But she couldn't keep her mouth shut. "Odd comment coming from you."

Drake blinked. With a smile, Everett lifted his cup to toast her.

The phone rang again. This time she didn't hesitate, and that told her something.

Both men studied her as she went through the standard greeting. "Mr. Parker?" she repeated. At least she knew that was Everett. "May I ask who's calling?"

She blinked. And her mind went blank. "Uhm…" She wished there was a script for this. "If you don't mind waiting, I'll see if the Kingmaker is in." Frantically she searched for the Hold button, and her finger trembled as she pressed it. "I… It could be a crank call."

They waited expectantly.

"The White House switchboard? Asking Everett to hold for the President of the United States?"

Drake grinned. "I believe Rylee just figured out that we might be a little more than a two-ring circus." He finished her donut and brushed the crumbs off his hands.

"I'll take it in my office."

"About that…?"

Everett sighed.

"I haven't been trained how to transfer calls." She shrugged. "Not that I work here, anyway."

"You're keeping POTUS waiting." Drake pointed out the obvious. Then he spoke to Everett. "Go ahead. I'll handle it."

She offered the handset to Drake.

"You do it. I'm a good teacher."

He was concise and not at all impatient, reminding her of the man who'd been so tuned into her that her body responded perfectly.

After hearing Everett's phone ring in his office, she exhaled a breath she hadn't realized was strangling her. "That was really…"

"Yeah. It was."

Crap.

"Does the job appeal to you at all? Excite you, maybe?"

He was luring her into his carefully laid trap. She was under no illusions about what he was doing—toying with her, cat and mouse.

"I'm offering you a chance to help us grow."

Suddenly things became clear to her. Drake *was* a dick, but she wanted to help Everett regain his crown.

"It's only six months. Surely you can do that."

For Everett, maybe. She hoped it wasn't the eternity it promised to be.

❧

"I'm asking you again. Are you out of your motherfucking mind?"

All day, Everett had gone out of his way to avoid Drake. It had been nice to have Rylee in the meeting with Lorraine—even nicer that he'd gotten every penny he wanted out of her client, but Everett's absence had been noticeable.

Most of the day, his office door was closed.

He'd spent the last two hours of the day in the conference room with Rylee, and he'd shut the door then as well.

Instead of working on his cases, he'd prowled up and down the hallway, wondering what the hell they were talking about and hating every damn minute of it.

He could have gone home at six. But he didn't.

Instead he poured a shot of whiskey—from the Bonds stash; after all, today was more than worth celebrating—and waited to see Rylee.

She emerged first, her hair in a messy bun and secured by a pen and smiling in a way that had never been directed at him.

And probably would never be with the way he snarled at her.

A feeling that was as unfamiliar as it was unwelcome—envy—sniped at him.

She'd breezed into the reception area where he was sitting in one of the two chairs she'd placed in front of her desk.

After grabbing her bag, she'd given him a quick wave, but no formal goodnight, as she'd headed out.

So when they were alone and Everett confronted him, Drake's adrenaline slammed into overdrive.

"I assure you, I'm of sound mind. The hire isn't just strategic; it's brilliant." He named one of the law firms she'd worked at. "She worked at one of the top law firms in the country. She knows how they operate. You saw her in action today." And spent two hours and three minutes alone with her. "She's smart. Composed. The right person to help us grow."

"What the hell kind of game are you playing?"

"Not sure what you're talking about. Her resume came across my desk. Sight unseen, I hired her."

"You discussed every previous candidate with me."

"Sally quit yesterday. Neither of us expected that." He shrugged. "We needed someone urgently."

Everett grabbed the bottle and poured himself a glass. "And it just happened to be the woman you're obsessed with?"

"A fortunate coincidence."

"Don't believe in it. And neither do you."

"What's the problem? She's imminently qualified."

"And if she doesn't work out, you'll fire her?"

The back of Drake's neck itched. "Sure."

"You're a damn liar." Everett downed his drink in a single swallow. "You always adjust your tie when you're trapped. It's like a poker tell."

Drake slammed down his glass.

"You need to listen to reason. She's someone we played with and would like to again. You must terminate this contract immediately. And let her keep the signing bonus."

"No chance."

"We can't work with someone we want to fuck."

"There's no employee manual preventing fraternization."

"Lawyer-speak. Just because there's no written rule against it doesn't mean it's a good idea." Everett paused. "Don't dip your pen in the company ink."

"Crude." And didn't move him one little bit.

Everett shook his head in frustration. "You saw what happened to Allison."

The candidate Drake had helped destroy.

"She had a husband, kids. Her star was shining. She could have stayed in office for life, maybe run for President."

"Your point is…?"

"Anyone can be tempted to cross the line, Drake. *Anyone.* Even you."

"She signed an employment contract."

"You trapped her. With the money, with telling her you want her to be a team leader."

No secrets in this office. "I prefer the word enticed."

"In my realm, we call that spin. In other words, bullshit." Everett yanked off his already-loose tie. "This whole thing is fucking madness."

Drake allowed his silence to speak for itself. "You didn't seem to mind spending two hours with her."

"We had a pleasant conversation."

Pleasant? "What did you talk about?"

"None of your damn business."

Drake thoughtfully inclined his head to one side. "I thought we were partners."

"I thought so too. Let it torture you." He exhaled. "But I'll tell you this. I asked what she wanted out of a job, whether this was a good fit for her. What her dreams and aspirations were. What gives her fulfillment. Things you didn't consider."

When Drake didn't respond, Everett plowed ahead. "She's not from our world."

Which was part of what drew Drake to her. His soul craved her innocence. She wasn't capable of the jaded manipulations that had shredded his heart into ribbons.

"She can be hurt in ways we don't understand. At some point, you might try thinking about someone other than yourself."

He was thinking of her. She was perfect for him. For them.

"Today's not that day, is it?" Everett thumped down his glass, sloshing some of the liquid gold over the edge, not seeming to care that it wended its way across the desktop. "Let me guess. You set your sights on something, and the emotional cost to someone else is immaterial? Winning is everything."

"It's the *only* thing."

"I'll tell you this, Drake. You damage her emotions in any way, I will fucking destroy you."

The office door slammed behind Everett, and the wood shook in its frame.

Now that he was alone, Drake took her heart necklace out of his pocket and allowed it to dangle from his finger. Nothing was off-limits when it came to keeping Rylee D'Angelo.

CHAPTER SIX

"Holy shit."

Rylee grinned at Juliana's exclamation. *Holy shit* was right.

"Are you freaking kidding me? Last night you got a job for more money than you've ever made *and* started today?"

Rylee propped the phone between her ear and shoulder so she could continue to unpack her kitchen and talk to Juliana at the same time.

But keeping herself moving forward was a challenge.

She'd been tired when she woke up this morning, and she hadn't left the office until after six p.m.

"Dish. I want all the details."

On some level, she was trying to sort all that through herself. From the moment she'd seen Drake perched on the edge of her desk, her mind had been reeling. Trying to buy time, she changed the subject. "You haven't told me how New York is."

"Amazing!" Even across the fourteen hundred air miles that separated them, Juliana's enthusiasm was contagious. "I haven't had much opportunity to get out, but the energy. I don't need caffeine anymore; I just soak in the vibe of the city. But I need someone to explore it with. Tell me you booked a ticket already?"

With her new job, affording the flight was more possible than it had been two days ago. But Rylee wasn't sure Drake would even allow her a day off. "And the company you work for?"

"Seems fine so far. It's been mostly orientation and onboarding."

Rylee laughed. K and G and Associates didn't believe in either of those things. As far as she could tell, they didn't even have an employee manual. Which, she supposed, allowed Drake to make things up as he went along.

"I'll start training in my department on Monday. Nine a.m. Such a reasonable time to start work. Better than the seven a.m. in Houston." Juliana paused, and it sounded as if she took a sip of something. No doubt her favorite wine. "Now back to you. I want to hear *all* the details. It was only a couple of days ago that you were freaking out about paying your bills."

"How much wine have you had? You're going to need it."

"I'm all ears."

"You remember the night we went to the Retreat right before you left?"

"And two delicious Dominants played with you? Then you ran away like Cinderella? Leaving your necklace behind?"

That was mostly true, and Rylee laughed. "Turns out they're my bosses."

"Wh...?" Juliana whistled. "Wait. Whoa. My mind is blown.

Rylee's also. In a couple of sentences, she summarized her first twenty minutes on the job, ending with dropping the cans of energy drink on the floor. To his credit, Drake had picked them up and stacked them in the fridge.

"So who are they? Are they millionaires like you guessed?"

"I just got home, and I haven't had time to google them yet. But…" She had zero doubt that they were at least millionaires. "They have to be."

"Billionaires?"

"Maybe." She dropped the last teaspoon into its slot in the silverware drawer, then slid it shut. One chore done. A thousand more to go.

"I can't believe you didn't quit on the spot."

"I was tempted."

"But the money?"

That was part of it. "I negotiated a signing bonus that was waiting on my desk. But mostly it was Everett. We had a long meeting this afternoon." Rylee paused. "I like him. He seems genuine." And maybe she was naive for thinking that. People didn't move in the highest echelons of government without being a power broker. He might have had a fall from grace, but the call from the White House proved how well respected he was.

"So what is your position?"

"Right now, it's executive assistant."

"You should be running the place."

Rylee appreciated her friend's loyalty. "That seems to be part of the plan."

"Oh?" In the background, Rylee heard a glug as if Juliana was refilling her glass. "I'm listening."

"Drake says the firm plans to grow."

"How many people right now?"

"Just them. Well, and me."

"Empires have been built with fewer people."

"They're supposedly having new offices built, and they

want to bring on other attorneys and staff." She paused. Now that she was saying it aloud, it seemed that maybe Drake had been trying to manipulate her with his comments. While she instinctively trusted Everett, she couldn't say the same for his partner. Especially after learning the way Drake operated behind the scenes to bring down Allison Danbury.

Then she'd sat in on his meeting with Lorraine James— who reminded Rylee of a beautiful barracuda.

Lorraine and Drake were so similar in their cutthroat approaches, Rylee wondered why the relationship had fallen apart. She couldn't imagine anyone more perfect for the dick.

At the end of the meeting, after she'd lost, Lorraine wouldn't shake his hand. Not that Rylee blamed the attorney. Drake's smile had been filled with triumph. Gloating was never a good look.

Watching him in action had been thrilling, and she'd been invigorated by seeing the master play at the top of his game. Part of her was undeniably attracted to that kind of energy.

Then Everett had called her into the conference room. And it had been like going from an electrical storm on the ocean to a peaceful sunset on a placid lake. Both were perfect in their own way.

Everett had taken a great interest in her goals and dreams, wanting to know what she wanted long-term for her career. Did being an operations manager appeal to her?

Then he went to the whiteboard and sketched out the plans they had in place for the future and assured her of the firm's financial stability. Each of them had brought ten million dollars in equity to the table to fund the growth they desired.

She'd been astounded that he'd trusted her with that information. After all, she hadn't signed a non-disclosure, something she couldn't believe Drake hadn't thought of.

"You got really quiet."

And she appreciated that Juliana had respected her silence. "It's a lot to work through."

"At least you have the weekend. And if you decide it's not for you, I'm sure Francesca will find you something else."

But it wouldn't be with the Kingmaker and the Dick.

"Are you going to play with them again?"

"No." Rylee paced the floor to work off some of the tension crawling through her. She had no intention of going to the Retreat again. "That would be stupid."

"And…?" Juliana laughed. "Knowing that in advance has never influenced any of my life choices. Especially where millionaire Dominants are concerned."

Rylee wished she could say she wouldn't be tempted. After all, her vulnerability where they were concerned was the main reason she'd fled. "Speaking of that… What happened with the Dom you played with?"

"Uhm…" Juliana took a gulp.

Now it was Rylee's turn to pry. "Do go on."

"He's coming for a visit."

Rylee squeed. "Really?"

"He wants to take me to a club in the city. And maybe we'll stay in Times Square."

"Take pictures, a thousand of them, and send them to me."

"You know it."

Together they said, "Pictures or it didn't happen!"

After dissolving into laughter, they wound down the conversation.

"You'd better keep me posted about your office romance."

"It's not an office romance." Rylee's protest was quick, but not convincing.

"Uh-huh. You mean not yet. Those two won't be able to keep their hands off you."

"I have no plan to sleep with the boss." She scowled. "Or bosses."

95

"Yeah." Juliana snickered. "I bet they don't think the same way you do."

With the way Drake had swept his gaze over her when she exited the conference room, she had to agree with her friend.

A shudder rippled through Rylee.

How in heaven was she supposed to resist the compelling draw of Drake Griffin?

Haunted by the question, Rylee was keyed up.

She managed to find a goblet, still packed. After unwrapping it from its packing material, she poured herself a glass of wine—which was about the only thing in her refrigerator.

So far, she'd only managed to put away about half of the items she needed to in order to make the kitchen functional. Sooner rather than later, she had to get organized. All week, she'd ordered takeout meals, and she preferred to cook for herself. It was much cheaper that way. And she was less likely to indulge in an after-dinner dessert, a craving she always succumbed to dining out.

Hoping to unwind, she took a bath, but once she was up to her chin in bubbles, her wicked thoughts returned to her bosses—and Dominants.

Despite the fact that it was nearly eleven o'clock, curiosity got the best of her. After drying off, dressing in a robe, and pouring a second glass of wine, she powered up her computer to find out everything she could about Drake and Everett.

The hundreds of articles kept her busy for hours.

Drake's breakup had been covered in *Scandalicious*—her favorite online gossip magazine—as had the fact Everett's fiancé dumped him after Allison's stunning election defeat.

There was another short article that mentioned the Zetas, a supposed secret society composed of some of the world's most influential people: artists, musicians, business and world leaders, billionaires, authors, celebrities, politicians, lawyers…kingmakers.

Members were referred to as Titans. The organization— that no one had been able to prove existed despite over a hundred years of rumors and conjecture—reportedly had Athena's owl as one of their symbols.

Her hand had frozen on her mouse as she thought back to the night at the Retreat. Had Drake's leather bag had an owl on the side?

Blinking, Rylee sat back. It had been so distinctive; there'd been no mistaking it.

Just who the hell was she working for?

These were no ordinary men. Their lifestyles and the people they knew were foreign to her. And the chance to find out more, be part of whatever their grand plans were, made her heart race. This was an incredible opportunity, maybe once in a lifetime. And even if she left their employ at the end of the six months, she would have incredible experience, a much broader resume, and—potentially—have connections that might lead to a more powerful position.

Even at the end of the business day and talking to Everett, she'd been unsure she wanted to continue to work for K and G and Associates.

But right now? She was all in.

～

The obnoxious, unwelcome shrill of the phone tore a jagged path through Rylee's dreams.

Scowling, she buried the phone beneath her pillow as if that would make it shut up.

But then blessed silence fell, and she drifted back off.

Only to be brutally ripped from the sweetness of sleep one more time. Who the hell was it at—she turned on her side to blearily glance at the bedside clock—the unholy hour of 6:07 a.m. on a Saturday morning?

A misdial or spam call, no doubt.

She dug for the phone and hit a hot button on the side to silence the horrible sound.

Finally she exhaled as the room fell silent.

A few minutes later, the damn phone shrilled again.

She snatched up the device and blinked several times to bring the words on the screen into focus.

K and G and Ass.

Which was appropriate.

But what the actual hell?

Her weekends belonged to her. And she had a million things to do, including trying to figure out how to finish putting her bookcases together so the living room wasn't a disaster waiting to happen.

With a sigh, she swiped the green button. She knew the obnoxious caller wasn't Everett. *"What?"*

"Where are you?"

She scowled. "What do you mean where am I? It's Saturday morning. Before dawn." Or at least she thought it was. But she'd be damned if she'd tell him she was in bed. No way was she inviting further conversation along those lines.

"We're interviewing a big client this morning, and we need you here."

"You can't be serious."

"Your employment agreement does say other responsibilities as directed."

Jesus. She'd never work for a lawyer again. "It doesn't say anything about nights or weekends."

"Actually it does."

"Are you serious?" She listened closely to his response, trying to detect even the barest hint of humor.

"I am."

There was no joking in Drake Griffin's baritone. "I'll send a car for you since you're already late."

"Late? This is earlier than a weekday."

"Duty calls. How much time do you need?"

"An hour and a half."

"Forty-five minutes it is."

Annoyed as hell, Rylee sighed.

"The coffee shop in the building is closed today. So please make other arrangements for our beverages."

No wonder the firm couldn't keep anyone employed. They weren't just billionaire bosses. They were billionaire bossholes.

Forty minutes later, her phone chimed with a message notifying her that her car was waiting downstairs. The ride would save her time parking and walking to the high-rise—and it would help her wallet. She'd also have the luxury of being able to order the coffee while someone else drove.

Wearing a skirt and heels—because she was going to be included in a big meeting—she hurried down the stairs.

And she stopped for a second.

This wasn't an ordinary Uber; it was a massive black SUV with a driver wearing a suit and cap. The vehicle belonged in River Oaks or Tanglewood, not her apartment complex.

"Ms. D'Angelo?"

Pretending as if she'd done this a hundred times, she nodded as he doffed his hat and opened the door for her.

She had to hitch up her skirt a little and accept the driver's arm to step up onto the running board. The next time Drake sent a car for her, she'd wear a skirt that didn't conform to her rear as if it had been poured on.

The leather was like butter and the compartment cool, which was more than welcome on this outrageously humid morning.

"Ready, ma'am?"

"We have to stop for coffee."

"Mr. Griffin doesn't function without it."

"Are you his personal driver?"

He met her gaze in the rearview mirror. "On the days he requires me."

From his tone, she knew he'd reveal no more information about his employer.

"Any particular place in mind, Ms. D'Angelo?"

"Rylee, please."

"Theodore."

"Give me a second to look it up. It's not far." She opened her app and read him the address of her preferred location. "What kind of coffee do you drink?"

"Ma'am?"

"Mr. Griffin told me to get you one."

"Pardon me, ma'am, if I have a difficult time believing that."

So evidently everyone thought Drake was a dick.

She looked up from her phone screen where she was entering the order. "You look like a venti white mocha man to me, Theodore."

He laughed. "Iced."

Had she actually guessed? Or was he being polite?

Yesterday Everett informed her that she had access to petty cash to reimburse coffee and food orders.

For a moment, she drummed her fingers on the seat next to her as she waged an internal debate. It lasted about three seconds before she caved, adding a chocolate donut to the order to make up for the one that was stolen the day before.

Then she decided to make it two.

But, since she had no idea how long it might be until lunch, she ordered four breakfast sandwiches and some other assorted pastries—all of which she liked.

When she reached the screen to confirm the order, Rylee winced.

Sixty-seven dollars and twelve cents.

After hitting the button to place the order, she added a nice tip. Maybe that would teach Drake not to send her on the morning coffee runs.

While Theodore double parked, she ran in to gather the tray of drinks and bags of treats.

Grinning, the driver opened the door for her. "I like your style, ma'am."

"Rylee," she corrected for the second time. "The one on that corner"—she nodded—"is yours."

While she balanced the tray, he plucked his out and placed it in a cup holder before taking the rest of them from her so that she could scramble onto the back seat.

Having help and not having to worry about finding and paying for parking was the ultimate luxury.

If the partners wanted her to stay beyond her six-month obligation, maybe she'd ask for a driver of her own.

She grinned. It was worth a try.

As Theodore eased into traffic, she slid her drink into its safe place, then reached into the bag and fished out one of the still-steaming sandwiches. She leaned forward and reached over the front seat. "For you."

Once again he met her gaze. "You're going to spoil me, Rylee."

"Compliments of Drake."

"I see."

While the vehicle glided through the almost-empty streets, she enjoyed every bite of her donut—made better from waiting a whole day for it.

Since the building was secured on Saturdays and no one had thought to get her a badge, Drake had to come down to sign her in.

He scowled. "Did you buy out the store?"

"Only one of them." She offered him the bags to carry.

In the elevator, he stood so close it unnerved her, so she took a step away from him then balanced the beverage tray as she pretended to rummage through her bag. Avoided conversation that way as well.

Everett was standing in the office, shirtsleeves turned back, with no tie on. He at least greeted her with a smile.

"Shall we get started?" Drake led the way to the conference room.

Cans of energy drinks were already popped open on the table. Just how long had they been at work?

Everett slid a pack of papers toward her. One of them was crumpled a little. "Copier jammed." He shrugged an apology. "Don't know how to fix it."

Another chore for her. Job security, she supposed, divvying up the cups and offering each man a sandwich before placing the second chocolate donut on a napkin in front of herself.

Drake eyed her. "Is there another one of those?"

"Afraid not." She took a bite. "But I did bring an assortment of other goodies for you to choose from."

Then ignoring him, she picked up the dossier Everett provided.

One of the local Harris County political parties thought Lowell McCoy was a potential candidate for mayor. Well liked and a judge, he'd presided over a high-profile murder trial that had garnered national coverage and not all of it favorable. He was known as being tough on crime, but that didn't always fly well with voters, especially since he was rumored to have wielded his influence to get his own kid out of trouble. And he was now going through a messy divorce.

"I met with him a couple of weeks ago. Likeable enough, which is one of the few things in his favor. I want both of you to talk to him. Drake's working on a deep background check. Our version of oppo research."

She frowned.

"Opposition. What his opponents will be searching for. If there's anything there, I want to find it first. And Drake—"

He nodded.

"Excels at it."

Evidently that was something to be proud of.

"We want to know where his allegiances lie. Who is he beholden to? Can we get him elected?"

Rylee moved her donut aside. "Do we want to?"

Everett shrugged.

"That's an idealist question, Rylee. Yesterday you said you were more of a realist."

Unflinchingly she met his gaze. "That's before I found out you worked to get a scum bucket elected to office."

Everett started to laugh then cleared his throat. "Well then."

Eyes blazing with that scary amber intensity, Drake leaned forward. "Everyone has secrets, Rylee. How deep are they buried?"

He unnerved her. It was as if he was no longer talking about the candidate.

Everrett broke the preternatural silence. "It only matters if you're running for office, and especially if you tout family values. A lot of damaging things can be spun or hidden."

"Buying silence?"

Both men shrugged.

"Scandals can be managed." Everett stood and crossed to the whiteboard that he'd wiped clean after their talk yesterday. He picked up a marker, but instead of uncapping it, he walked it through his fingers. "The trick is for us to know all the minutia ahead of time. Candidates, no matter how many offices they've held, are notorious at refusing to reveal their pasts."

"Not sure I blame them."

"The higher you climb, the more money is spent on oppo research. Think of a nominee for the Supreme Court. College yearbooks are scoured, classmates are spoken to. When their name is made public, people remember things. The right reporter with the right amount of money can make them talk. Pictures are worth a thousand words. Which is what took down Allison."

"I get it."

Drake took over the conversation. "We'll be meeting with the judge and a volunteer from the campaign who's driving and taking notes, an assistant of sorts. And he'll also have a political adviser with him who will be posturing. Because if Lowell hires us, that man will be demoted, if not fired. He's run some state campaigns, but mayor of Houston is a different beast. A lot of special interests at work."

Rylee broke off a piece of her donut. "And facing a popular incumbent."

Everett tossed the marker in the air. "Well done."

Since the trio was scheduled to arrive within thirty minutes, they all straightened the room. Then Rylee said she'd brew a pot of coffee. "You don't have a cleaning crew?"

"We're hoping our exec will hire one."

"You know, at some point, knowing what to do would make me a more valued team member."

Drake raised an eyebrow. "Figuring out what needs to be done and handling it would make you a more valued team member."

With a sharp inhalation, she absorbed the counter criticism. He'd scored a hit. "I'm going to need a part-time assistant."

"Then get one."

"You're serious?"

Without answering he left the room.

She watched him go. Then shaking her head, she met Everett's gaze. "Is he serious?"

"Does he look like a man who jokes around?"

"I have no idea how much authority I actually have."

"We want to grow. He hired you to do that."

And he'd dared her to impress him.

"You came back, even though it's a weekend, which tells both of us something, right?"

It did. She liked being challenged. And as much as she hated to admit it to herself, she liked being around both men. She hadn't been this vibrantly alive in so long she'd forgotten what it felt like.

"Despite my best efforts, I had no success in trying to get him to fire you last night."

She gasped. "Are you serious? You actually—"

"If you want out, you've got two choices, Rylee. Fuck up so bad he has no choice. Or quit. Otherwise the bastard doesn't intend to let you go."

CHAPTER SEVEN

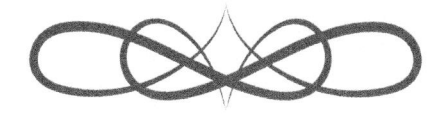

"Thoughts?"

Once again, Everett stood in front of the whiteboard.

The potential candidate and his entourage had left, taking their considerable energy with them.

She and her bosses had needed a ten-minute break, then reconvened for a post mortem on the meeting.

"Rylee?" Everett looked at her. "You go first."

"*Me?*"

"A woman's point of view is always welcome."

She took a breath. "This is vague..." Something about Lowell bothered her. "I can't quite figure it out, but he didn't feel authentic. Like he was putting on an act."

"Could have been."

"He was cold. And he never made eye contact with me."

"Interesting." Everett jotted her impression on the whiteboard. "Could be a weakness. If others spot it. But will they?"

"I just didn't connect with him. He's too polished. Too perfect. His answers were rote, and he didn't have any solid plans, just vague complaints about the current adminis-tration."

"Developing a platform would be part of our job."

"I guess I think he's doing it for political purposes, not because he's interested in the job or cares about the Bayou City. I mean, we have flooding in some areas. It's a big concern. He never mentioned it." *But criminals and being tough on crime? Even corruption? He was all over that.*

Drake spoke next. "I agree with Rylee. Betting she's right about his motivation. On the other hand, he'll look good on television."

"Hmm." She considered that. "That matters?"

"Yeah." Everett confirmed. "He's tall, broad. Which means he'll tower over the competition. A lot of times voters go for the candidate with the greatest physique."

"You're kidding right?"

"A study showed that the taller candidate in twenty-one presidential elections won... Want to guess the percentage?"

"Seventy?" When Everett shook his head, she guessed again. "Seventy-five?"

"Eighty."

She blinked.

"Can we count on that? Of course not." He shrugged. "But another study showed only two presidents were shorter than the average height. For their time period in history, of course. But it's something I don't discount without consid-eration."

"For example?"

"He's good looking. Keeps himself fit. Well spoken. After all, he's accustomed to commanding his own little fiefdom—his courtroom. The combination of those factors gives him an edge that some of his opponents might not have."

Everett focused on Drake. "Anything to add?"

"I think you've covered it. And Rylee has some interesting

insights. Are they exploitable? Will he come across as inauthentic on camera?" Drake shook his head. "One-on-one, maybe, but he's polished. Been on television enough that he's comfortable in front of the camera. He'll appear polished and confident. Believes he has righteousness on his side."

Rylee spoke up again. "Houston voters often go for someone who doesn't share his viewpoints."

"She's right." Everett returned to the table. "Political winds matter."

Drake jotted a note. "I'll have my team start digging. Because he's a public figure who's run for office, there's some info out there. But a cursory glance looks good—what he wants people to know because it resonates. Fifth generation Texan."

Rylee had no idea all these factors mattered so much to voters.

"Law degree from UT Austin."

"Instead of an Ivy League school?"

Everett answered. "He's running for office in the Great State of Texas. How much that matters in Houston is up for debate. To some, that will weigh in his favor. Certainly if he's aiming for governor, it'll play."

"Down the road, you'd like to handle that campaign?"

"If he can win. That's the question, isn't it? Can he raise the tens of millions of dollars it will take?"

She sank back in her chair. "Tens of millions?"

"Rough guess of fifty."

"The stakes are that high?"

"Likely fifteen million needed to run the mayoral campaign. In case of a runoff."

"This is shocking." Then she cocked her head to one side. "What does the Oracle say?"

"That political winds may be the biggest factor. And likeability."

"And he doesn't have that." She smiled. "The current mayor certainly does." A single mom, she was as likeable and warm as she was tough.

"Will she run again, though?" Everett threw out the question. "Or does she have higher ambitions? The president may be looking to her to fill a cabinet position."

"Was that what the call was about yesterday?"

"Sorry." Everett's smile was completely unapologetic. "I can't answer that."

All kinds of behind-the-scenes activity. "That's why we met today, isn't it? So no one was aware that he's considering a run."

"Or shopping for a campaign manager. We most certainly aren't the only firm he's talking to."

So being called in on a Saturday—or after hours—was most definitely not unusual.

Drake spoke up. "You ready to hire a tracker?"

"Yeah. We're still a couple of years out, but this election will be high-profile. National attention."

"I'll handle it."

"Anything else?" Everett studied them both. "Or should we pick this up again Monday morning?"

In that moment, she made a decision.

She liked this job. Enough, probably, to tolerate the world-class bosshole who'd hired her.

As the men gathered their belongings, Rylee spoke up. "Drake, I need you to go to the lobby with me so I can get a badge."

"We can do it on Monday."

She set her chin. "Do you want me to be part of the team or not?"

For the second time that day, Everett laughed.

Drake sighed. "When?"

"No time like the present. We have work to do." Since he

was glaring, she changed her tactics. "You're far too impor-tant for me to keep interrupting your schedule, making you run down to the lobby." She gave him a wide, bright smile. "Or carry bags of scones. But if that's how you want to spend your day…"

He scowled and led the way to the door. "Point taken."

Getting it handled took less than five minutes.

After she and Drake returned to the suite, she asked for the contact information for the firm's IT company.

"Have Everett handle it."

"Very good." She walked to Everett's office, knocked on the door, and then let herself in without waiting for an invitation.

"I'll need you to call the company who takes care of IT. I need an email address and access to all the computer files. Now, please."

Everett blinked. "You're relentless."

From the reception area, Drake called out, "Not so funny now, is it, partner?"

Within half an hour, she was in business. Except for one thing. She walked into Drake's office and placed her hands on his desk to ensure his attention. "I need a key."

"There's one somewhere in your desk. Middle drawer, maybe. Try that."

When she remained where she was, he looked up and met her gaze. "Anything else?" His voice was polite but curt with impatience.

"As a matter of fact, yes. I want to be added to the compa-ny's checking account."

Drake sat back "You…?"

"You want me to handle things? Then you'll provide the resources for me to be effective in my position."

"Fucking bravo, Rylee." He grinned. "Anything else?"

"Yes. I want a credit card."

"I'll handle it on Monday."

"No reason to wait. They have twenty-four-hour customer service." She smiled. She'd found statements in the files and already called to find out what was required. "I checked."

He exhaled.

She smiled sunnily. "A little sacrifice today will make your future easier. After all, we're at work on a Saturday, we might as well make the hours count. Don't you agree?" She stood there while he placed the call and made the arrangements. When he was wrapping up, she spoke again. "Have it overnighted."

Shaking his head, he made the request. Then after hanging up, he regarded her again. "Anything else?"

"I hate open loops. They cause distraction and take away from productivity."

"What loop shall we close, pray tell?"

"We need to calendar the time we'll meet up at the bank on Monday. No doubt I'll need to fill out a signature card."

He clapped—literally applauding her.

Dumbfounded, she stood there, unmoving, unsure how to react. In her entire life, no one had ever shown her this kind of approval.

"This is what I saw in your resume and what I was told when I checked your references. You're a hard worker. Resourceful enough to finish your previous project ahead of schedule even though it meant you were out of a job. Frankly, Rylee, you rose to the challenge. You're impressing the hell out of me."

His reaction was every bit as potent as a drug, and she fed off its power. After she shook her head to clear it, she returned to the topic at hand. "So what time?"

"We have a private banker. He'll bring the card to us."

"You'll notify him that he needs to stop by? Or shall I?"

"I'll do it."

When she continued to stand there, unmoving, he sighed and took out his cell phone. A minute later, his device pinged, and he looked at her. "Ten a.m. satisfactory, Ms. D'Angelo?"

She nodded. "I'll add it to the schedule. If I require anything else, I'll let you know."

"I'm quite sure you will." He smiled and not one of the fake, dangerous ones that were so familiar. This was deep, toying around the corners of his eyes, making him less ferocious and much more accessible.

The other Drake might turn her on, but she recognized this one was far more dangerous. A charming Drake might find his way into her heart.

Still, pleased, she wasn't sure whether she walked or floated back to her desk.

Now that the IT company had worked their magic, she had access to the firm's scheduling software. After setting a reminder about the meeting with the banker for both her and Drake, she emailed Francesca requesting resumes from people who were looking for part-time work. Finally Rylee made arrangements for a janitorial service that was available to start on Tuesday.

At least now the offices would look a little more reputable, fitting the image they should be presenting to the world.

When she was done organizing her desk, she informed Drake she needed a ride home.

"Theodore is waiting. Text him."

She flashed him a smile. "Thank you."

"Pleasing you, Rylee, is *my* greatest pleasure."

Just like that, her world flipped upside down again. Resisting his charms would require all her willpower.

She returned home with momentum still zipping through her.

After changing out of her skirt and into leggings, she made herself a grilled cheese sandwich, finished unpacking the kitchen, and then moved on to the bathroom. Getting organized at work was inspiring her in other areas.

She told herself it had nothing to do with Drake's approval, but a tiny voice whispered that she was fibbing to herself.

That night, she slept better than she had in weeks, if not months, and woke up without an alarm before seven a.m.—unheard of on a Sunday.

Yesterday's enthusiasm still energizing her, Rylee ignored the coffeepot in favor of pulling on a pair of shorts and a lightweight shirt before heading to the apartment complex's workout space.

Twenty minutes later, she hit the Stop button on the treadmill. That was definitely more than enough cardio for someone who hadn't looked at a piece of exercise equipment in years.

Back inside her home, she treated herself to coffee before throwing in a pile of laundry, paying bills, and unpacking the remaining boxes of clothes in her bedroom.

By noon, with the exception of the confounding set of bookcases, her entire house was exactly the way she wanted it.

After spending another few minutes with the assembly instructions that might as well have been in a foreign language, she gave into frustration and took a shower. Then she debated what to do with the rest of her afternoon.

If Juliana still lived in town, no doubt they'd get together, enjoy lunch and maybe a coffee before browsing some shops in the Heights. But going out alone didn't appeal to Rylee.

So instead, she dressed in a fresh pair of leggings, tennis

shoes, and a soft, snuggly T-shirt before pulling her hair into a ponytail, applying the barest amount of foundation and mascara, then grabbing her bag as she headed to the office.

Although the law firm was moving, it could be months. And finding everything she needed would ensure the company operated smoothly in the interim.

Because it was already a habit, she stopped to grab a coffee. But because she'd worked out—well, sort of—and surely that was the start of a good habit, she skipped the donut.

Inside the high-rise, she flashed her ID to the security guard and signed the log before opting for the stairwell instead of the elevator.

As she enjoyed her drink, she scanned her email. Francesca had already sent along several resumes with letters of reference attached. She'd also highlighted her recommended choice.

Had she done the same for Drake?

And if so, had Rylee's name been at the top, or had he kept looking until he found hers?

She agreed with Francesca's recommendation—a woman with years of experience who was available to work fulltime on occasion if needed. If her bosses truly wanted her to be more of an executive, then Rylee needed someone reliable who could fill in.

After responding that she'd like to set up and interview and suggesting a few different times, she answered a call from the building security guard informing her a package was waiting for her in the lobby.

Her credit card.

Just in time because she wanted to order a desk and chair for the new hire. Then she changed her mind. The part-timer could have the desk Rylee currently occupied. She'd take the office the owners were currently using to workout. There was enough space in the copy and supply room for their workout bench and exercise bike. And if Drake didn't like it, he could move it to his office.

Grinning, she checked the budget in the accounting program. There was a healthy amount available for furniture —no doubt because they were building new offices. Anything she purchased could be taken with them.

She jogged down the stairs to grab her card. Then after settling in to activate it and check the limit, she started shopping.

Spending someone else's money was much more satisfying than she imagined.

Her coffee was empty by the time she made her decision, something serviceable, but not as masculine as the pieces in Everett and Drake's offices. Before confirming the purchase, she added a framed print and some décor to the order. Then she checked the final box, paying for setup, something she should have done for her own bookcases.

After rubbing her hands together, she decided to tackle the next big project. She was dragging the weight bench into the copy room when the main office door slammed, making her jump.

She scowled, expecting to have space to herself on a Sunday.

"What the actual…"

Freezing in spot, she looked up to take in Drake's puzzled frown, and his gorgeous body and overwhelming presence.

"Rylee? What are you doing here?" He loosened his tie as he shook his head. "Belay that. I can see what you're doing. A better question is why?"

"I'm rearranging so that there's room for my furniture when it's delivered later in the week."

"Your…"

Since he'd obviously heard her, she didn't respond. Instead she resumed dragging the bench.

"Stop that immediately."

"I'm working here, Drake."

"I said stop." His voice was a whiplash, authoritative and uncompromising, and she knew better than to argue.

Straightening, she met his gaze.

"I'll do that."

She blew out a breath. For a moment she thought he'd refuse to let her have that office.

"When you're presented with a challenge, you accept it."

"I'll take that as a compliment." Even if he didn't mean it that way.

He removed his jacket and offered it to her.

She wished she hadn't automatically accepted. His spicy, crisp scent clung to the warm fabric, reminding her of the night at the club when they'd been so intimately connected.

"So you expect me to workout in this room that has no window and crappy air conditioning?"

"Better than me calling it home." She offered a cheeky grin.

"I assume this means you're turning over your desk to a new hire?"

Whom she'd do a better job of training. "Your directive was to grow the company."

"Having more business to support it first would be ideal."

"Then sign some new clients. Settle some cases."

Temper flashed behind his eyes.

"Sir."

He shook his head. "You play dangerously, Ms. D'Angelo."

Refusing to cower, she responded in kind. "Mmm."

In the end, he opted to move the exercise bike to his office. "Better choice anyway."

In only a few minutes, the room was empty, ready for the

cleaning crew to arrive. And—feeling as if her hands had been singed—she'd returned his jacket.

It was already after four when she wrapped up for the day. As a courtesy, she knocked on Drake's door to let him know she was leaving.

"What plans do you have?"

Why are you asking? To be friendly? Or to encourage her to stay at work a little longer? Neither he nor Everett seemed to have a clue that business should ever stop. "Fighting with my bookcases."

When he drew his eyebrows together, she clarified. "I have a new apartment. I've spent the better part of a week trying to put together the darn things. Honestly I think that's part of the reason I came in today." She laughed. "Procrastination from the frustration."

"I'll handle it." He stood and snatched his jacket from the back of the chair.

"Uh." That darn fight-or-flight instinct once more left her glued to her spot, eyes wide. "I'm sure I can figure it out."

"And how long did you say you've been trying to put them together?"

She exhaled.

"It's obvious you like having things settled."

Rylee couldn't argue with that.

"You can ride with me."

"Drake… Really…"

"Unless you've got a secret lover hiding in your house, this isn't open for negotiation."

His absurd statement made her laugh.

"Let's go."

"But…"

He waited her out.

"Another time, maybe? I have my car."

"Fortunately for you, I'm pretty good with a GPS." He took a step toward her. "Or following you."

Her breath threatened to choke her. Arguing with him would be futile—that much she recognized.

Maybe he could get everything handled and she could send him on his way. No doubt he had plans for the night ahead. Maybe even visiting the Retreat?

Where had that awful thought come from? And why did it hurt so bad?

The drive home seemed to take much less time than usual.

He followed her up the flight of stairs, and she was uncomfortable having him see how she lived. The apartment was all she could afford—maybe even more than that—yet she was sure it was far beneath what he expected.

Once they were inside, he removed his jacket and tossed it over the back of the couch as casually as if it were his own place. Then he followed her toward the kitchen, not that it was more than a few steps. He pulled back a stool from the island and took a seat. "I like it. It's comfortable."

Which was a kind word for overrun with belongings. And how had she never noticed how low the ceilings were until now? "Thanks, it's…" Not much, but a step up from the way she was raised. "I appreciate your help."

"Anything for you, Rylee."

Even manual labor, it seemed.

"I can't offer you many choices of beverages. I still haven't gone to the grocery store or made a liquor store run. Wine, maybe? Though I have to warn you it's not up to your usual standards."

"I'm not a snob."

Rylee allowed his lie to hang between them, unchallenged. "You might want to skip it. It was on sale, the world's finest cardboard-aux."

"Guessing that means it comes in a box?" He grinned.

"With is very own spigot even."

"In that case, yeah. I'll have a glass."

"You can't be serious."

"It'll take me back to school. In college, one of the frat brothers would hold the box in the air, and we'd take turns drinking from the dispenser."

"Eww." She shuddered as she shook her head. "That's sounds dangerous."

"It was. One of my more regrettable decisions among many to be sure."

To his credit, he took a couple of drinks before sliding the glass to the side.

"Memories?" She laughed.

"Yeah. Anyway, let's see what you've got."

"Besides a mess?"

Still in his tie and shirt, he sat on the floor. "You're right. It's a mess."

But his tone was light.

"I warned you."

"So you did."

He came close to removing every screw she'd placed. "A couple of things are backward."

"That'll do it."

In the end, it took him less than fifteen minutes—and zero curse words—to have it fully functioning.

"You made that look easy."

"Well…"

"Don't rub it in. It was easy for you, an absolute nightmare for me."

"Happy to help anytime. All you have to do is ask. And I mean that."

"I appreciate this. You're a godsend, Drake."

"So thank me."

Oh God. What…? Had she misheard? She had to have misheard. No way was her boss propositioning her.

His gaze was hypnotic, and she couldn't look away. "Look, Mr. Griffin, I appreciate what you did, but—"

"Have dinner with me."

She blinked.

Regarding her, he tipped his head to one side. "You didn't think I was suggesting something else?"

He knew exactly where her mind had gone, precisely because he'd led her there.

"We're both hungry. There has to be some local place you've been wanting to try."

Damn him. On cue, her stomach growled. "I'm sure it's not to your taste any more than the wine was, but there's a nearby pizza parlor. Supposedly it's authentic. The family is from Sicily via New York."

"Let's go."

"Look, Drake."

He grabbed his jacket and shrugged into it. "Quit under-estimating me, Rylee. It's starting to piss me off."

"I've seen your car." Though his comment stung, she didn't back down. "You have a driver. Your own law practice."

"And you don't know a goddamn thing about me. So quit fucking pretending you do." A tiny pulse ticked in his temple, something she'd never seen from him before. "I mean it that you're starting to piss me off. This is a line you don't want to cross. Now grab your bag."

With a few clipped, carefully chosen sentences, he'd sucked the energy from the room.

"Forgive me if I find your…invitation lacking."

Sighing he dragged a hand through his hair, leaving him disheveled and more vulnerable. "Look. I apologize. You have ideas and opinions of me that frustrate the hell out of me."

"I've seen you in action, Mr. Play-to-Win."

"And has it ever occurred to you to find out why?"

Pain was lanced in his eyes.

"No. You haven't. You believe I was born with all the advantages, right? That I won the sperm lottery and was born into a billionaire family and enjoyed a luxurious childhood."

Since he was exactly right, she pressed her lips together instead of refuting his assumption.

"I'm the result of a one-night stand."

Her mind reeled.

"My mother was a cocktail waitress that he randomly fucked. It wasn't until her deathbed that I got my father's name out of her. I was eighteen. In all those years, he'd never accepted a call from her. He was protected by an army of lawyers and associates who never let her near him. All this means Jerome McNichols never paid a dime of child support. My mother and I lived in something close to poverty. I think we received government assistance, though she never said. That, Ms. D'Angelo, is why I went to law school. So I could sue the motherfucker for what he owed me and my mother."

She sank against the kitchen counter. "I had no idea."

"Of course not. I don't broadcast it. And McNichols paid plenty of money to ensure no one spoke to the press. So yeah, I remember the cardboard-aux being fancy. Pizza being an occasional treat. And I'm not ashamed of my roots. It made me what I am. Focused. Furious. And wanting to right the wrongs of the world. Did you ever look up the cases I take? Maybe you should."

"Drake…" Rylee had never been more wrong about some-one, something in her life, and humiliation threatened to tear her apart. "I'm sorry."

"Apology accepted. But spare me your pity. I don't need it. I don't want it."

She'd never met anyone like him.

"And now can we go get a pizza? With double cheese. It costs extra. And until I had my first victory, I hadn't been able to afford it."

She was capable of denying him nothing. "If you can forgive me?"

"It's not required. You just see what's on the surface and make those facts fit your view of the world."

His assessment stung, humbling her.

"And I'll buy the best bottle of wine they have."

She gave him a small smile that faded quickly. In his position she might not be so generous.

"For the love of God, Rylee, go with me or tell me where the restaurant is so I can go alone."

In the end, she grabbed her bag. Despite the heat and humidity that was like wearing a warm, wet blanket, they walked to the pizza parlor.

True to his word, he ordered the largest pizza with double cheese and extra pepperoni, and salads for two.

The wine was exquisite and more than the cost of five pizzas.

Once they were alone, he shrugged out of his jacket and turned back his shirtsleeves.

Every time she saw him, she was astounded anew by his attractiveness and strength. Her thoughts scattered. Being alone with him always slammed her libido into overdrive.

"Now that you know my past, tell me more about you." He stretched his arm across the back of the booth, and his fingertips almost touched her shoulder.

Uncomfortable talking about herself, she wiggled around. "My dad passed when I was small. No life insurance. Until then, my mom hadn't worked, so we struggled, but I was loved. She did well in her job, and right as I was graduating from high school, she was offered a transfer to Chicago." Though they spoke often, Rylee missed her mom and wanted to take a trip to see her soon. Even if it was an overnight visit. "Since I had friends here, I opted to stay in Houston. Found some roommates, but we lost the lease. One friend is living with her fiancé. The other took a job in New York City. I'm hoping to go see her soon. If my boss lets me have some time off."

He grinned, serving her another slice of pizza that she didn't need. But it tasted so good, hot, and ooey gooey, that she couldn't resist picking it up.

"I'm told he's an asshole."

"Really?" She fake-gasped. "I've heard that too."

The evening with him was more enjoyable than she could have ever imagined. They walked back in companionable silence, having shared a dessert. The sun had long ago set, and the first stars twinkled overhead.

He walked her up the stairs. Then, when she unlocked the door, he leaned forward and tucked a wisp of hair behind her ear. "Thank you for joining me. I had a wonderful evening."

It was magical.

He stood close, then closer.

Her heartrate increased. The moment was right and inevitable. "Drake…"

He brushed his thumb across her mouth. Mesmerized by the light touch, she parted her lips for him.

Stunning her, he took a slight step back and dropped his hand into his pocket.

"Don't wear leggings again."

"What?" She shook her head.

"I need to keep my hands off you and control my impulse to spank your hot ass. And you're making it difficult as hell."

Drake reached behind her to open the door. "Good night, Rylee."

After what had just happened, everything they shared, he was dismissing her? How was this even possible?

"Make sure you think about me this evening."

This one and every one that followed. And now, tormented, she'd be unable to sleep. With the way his nefarious mind worked, that was likely his intent.

When he took another step back, she turned, walked into the house, and slid the lock home. Drake Griffin was no doubt the most maddening, confounding man on the face of the planet.

And damn it all, she was falling in love with him.

CHAPTER EIGHT

"What are your impressions of Marcy?"

Across the massive dining room in the three-bedroom suite she shared with her bosses, Rylee looked at Everett and carefully considered her answer. In the almost three months since she'd joined the team, her life had changed dramatically.

Her money nightmares were behind her, and she was planning a trip to New York to see Juliana, who was loving the Big Apple. Rylee had hired Linda, the admin recommended by Francesca. Linda was a perfect, no-nonsense, and take-charge, completely unfazed by Everett and Drake's bosshole ways. Nothing rattled her, which made her a godsend.

Recently when they realized they needed her to become a fulltime employee, Linda had agreed, freeing up Rylee to handle other things.

At some point every day, she donned a hardhat and headed to their new building, which was still a construction site. Drake and Everett had abdicated the project, leaving the details to her, including carpeting, furnishings, even paint and trim choices. Fortunately the project manager had recommended an excellent interior decorator, and Rylee was working closely with him. They spent hours shopping and going through samples, and since she was in charge, she gave herself first choice of office space.

When Rylee wasn't occupied with that, she traveled with either Drake or Everett, and sometimes both. When that happened, they often regrouped at the end of the day in their suite rather than in a restaurant. They could be more casual, spread out their computers and papers, and not be concerned about being interrupted, overheard, or seen.

The presidential suite at the Sterling Prestige Austin was incredible. And no wonder. It was situated close to the state capitol, and it hosted a lot of luminaries and politicians who appreciated finer touches. The place was filled with luxurious cherrywood, high-end marble, unbelievably comfortable padded dining chairs, and a living room sofa she sank into and never wanted to leave.

Since it was the end of a whirlwind two-day bus tour with Marcy, who was exploring a run for congress, Rylee had kicked off her shoes, exchanged her skirt for leggings and her blouse for a for a soft tank top, and was sipping a superb red wine from a Waterford goblet. They were sharing a charcutier board, and they planned to order a late dinner when Drake returned from his meeting with Altair.

"You're hesitating." Over the rim of his glass, Everett studied her. "Why? Doubts about Marcy's viability?"

Rylee appreciated that Everett always sought her opinions. Over the time they'd spent together, she'd learned a lot, yet the more she knew, the more she realized how complex politics really was. Being called the Oracle was not something to be taken lightly. More and more she realized how badly the press had treated him after Allison Danbury's defeat. One headline had screamed, *Kingmaker Dethroned*.

An indiscretion—from the candidate, not him—had unfairly tarnished his reputation.

"Rylee?"

"It's…" Since the evening where Drake had pointed out how horribly she'd mischaracterized him and realizing how the nonstop gossip machine churned—demanding new, even more salacious rumors and conjecture—she'd been much more hesitant to rush to judgment. Yet no one understood that, or her complex relationship with Drake, better than Everett. "I'm trying to be more thoughtful." Well, unless she saw an obvious flaw. And Everett had almost always noted it himself first. "When I first met Drake, I made sweeping assumptions about him and the way he was raised. It's embarrassing to admit how wrong I was."

Everett snagged a piece of cheese. "He's still an asshole."

"Bosshole." She grinned.

He laughed. "Is that what you call him?"

"Well, sometimes both of you."

He blinked. "Me?"

"You have your moments."

"I'm wounded." He placed a hand to his heart.

Though he had legendary patience, even he had limits. Sometimes candidates pushed him too far, and he snapped. Then heaven help anyone in his path.

She grabbed an olive and popped it into her mouth. "Has he been like this the whole time you've known him?"

"No. He's worse than he used to be."

Rylee figured it was the situation with his father that turned him into the beast who was single mindedly focused on winning.

"It was Lorraine."

His ex. Waiting for Everett to go on, Rylee turned toward him a little more.

"She did a number on him."

"In what way?"

"It turns out she used him." Then he sighed. "Look, he needs to tell you this himself."

"You've intrigued me."

"Suffice it to say, he's opted never to love again."

Never love again? Were Everett's words a statement or a warning?

"It's his story. "

She nodded, understanding. Rylee hadn't been exactly forthcoming either. Working for the pair had gotten easier in some ways and more difficult in others. She knew her responsibilities and executed them well. Yet sexual tension continually crawled through her.

One evening, she and Drake had caught a late flight from the West Coast, putting them on the tarmac in Houston after three a.m. Horrifying her, she'd fallen asleep on his shoulder in the back of his comfortable SUV. Instead of waking her, he'd wrapped his arm around her.

He'd walked her to her apartment, taken off her skirt and blouse—despite her half-hearted, yawn-interrupted protests—then lightly kissed her forehead before leaving. She'd slept hard for six straight hours and had awakened with a smile.

He was often that solicitous, and it was maddening. She wanted him every bit as much as she wanted *not* to want him. One thing was certain—she was tired of his sweet, butterfly-like kisses.

She'd taken to traveling with her vibrator just so she wasn't continually distracted. "In that case, tell me about you."

"Me?" Everett echoed.

"Okay, so…" She paused for a second. "I shouldn't admit this…"

"Now you've got me intrigued."

"Scandalicious—"

He groaned.

"Scandalicious had a report of your engagement and a breakup. And no other details."

"Nothing much to report." But his eyes had clouded, and that wasn't like him.

She frowned. "I shouldn't have asked. Sorry."

"No. It's fair." Though he stared at his almost-full glass, he didn't touch it. "Sheryl wanted to marry a winner. When my star was ascending, she was happy." He scoffed. "Then came the Allison debacle. As things unwound, Sheryl became agitated, picking fights when I got home. How could I work with someone who would behave that way?" After a short pause, he shook his head and went on. "A million things like that, questioning my integrity because my candidate was human."

"Not what you needed."

"That's the truth." He pushed back his chair and stood, pacing to the window. "You haven't been there on election night yet, when we're waiting for results."

The *yet* part of his sentence reverberated in her. Her employment agreement stipulated six months. And none of them had discussed a future beyond that. She was days away from receiving her first five-thousand-dollar bonus. But that also meant she was nearing the end of her term.

"For local elections, there may be a watch party for any number of people who are running. A ballroom at a hotel, for example. Including this one. There will be booths or tables for all candidates, with televisions everywhere, all tuned to pundits. A generally festive area—or gloomy one—with a bar and food."

She nodded.

"On a statewide or national election, there may be individual watch parties hosted by the candidate themselves. And that was the case with Allison. We were at one hotel. Her opponent at another. We had a big celebration planned, and thousands of her supporters were in attendance, signs, balloons. Early results were in, and we had reason to be optimistic. She'd pulled it off once before."

Rylee remembered seeing a news clip at the end of that evening—including the heart-wrenching tears of some of her voters.

"Then it became obvious, undeniable. All of us were in shock because the turnaround had been so swift. Allison hadn't prepared a concession speech. Two weeks before, losing had been unthinkable." He paced, no doubt not the first person to do so in this space. "I went back to my room with her speechwriter, and we came up with something. Then Allison came to my room to call Finglas. Sheryl was at the bottom of her first bottle of champagne at that point— the one she'd ordered for our late-night victory celebration. The rest of us returned to the ballroom but Sheryl remained behind."

Rylee nodded.

"Signs were discarded. Disappointment tore through the place. We had thousands of balloons filled, ready to drop, a band hired, the room booked until one a.m." He sighed. "We wasted a ton of money and resources, none of which were needed. The campaign was my first meaningful loss."

Months, maybe even years of work, for nothing. "Was it a learning experience?"

"I don't know about that. Humbling, yes. Kneecapping. Ego damaging. Humiliating. Until then, there had been nothing I couldn't spin. Given enough time, I still believe she could have survived it. We would have been able to find something to use against Finglas." He lifted a shoulder. "The man opens his mouth enough to give us plenty of material in future campaigns."

"You'll work with someone against him?"

"In a heartbeat. I've got something to prove."

In him, she saw the same resolve and attitude that was familiar from Drake.

"So what about Sheryl?"

"That disaster." He shook his head. "After the concession speech—which Allison went off-script on—I spent time with her and her family. But it became obvious they didn't want or need me around. Maybe I shouldn't be surprised that I'm still waiting for my final check."

That part, she'd never considered. It wasn't just the candidate who lost, it was the advisers and manager. Maybe all the funds had been expended. And donors didn't rush to refill the coffers of the defeated. "Is there anything you can do to collect?"

"I can make more money."

"Something you're clearly good at."

"I'll take that as a compliment."

She remained silent, watching him, waiting for him to go on.

Eventually he did. "Wallowing in the black hole of defeat, I went back to my room. Sheryl was gone. She left two empty bottles of champagne and a note telling me that she wanted to marry a winner."

"Holy…" Rylee blinked. "You're kidding me?" But with the stricken look on his face, she knew he wasn't joking. "I'm sorry. No one deserves that. That's what marriage is about, right? Being there for each other, no matter what. Good times and in bad?"

"That was my expectation. But…" He gave a fatalistic shrug. "Better I found out beforehand, right? She kept the ring. God knows how much a divorce would have cost me. *That* was a learning experience." He leveled his gaze at her. Daggers, dark and stormy, lay in his gray eyes. She'd never seen that kind of resoluteness in him before. "Any woman I propose to in the future will have loyalty and integrity beyond question."

Silence hung on the air.

"She'd be someone very much like you, Rylee."

Breath was yanked from her lungs, and she wrapped her arms around herself. *Someone like me?*

He remained where he was, halfway across the room.

How was she supposed to react? It wasn't just Drake she loved; it was Everett as well. Which was a problem. Dating, fucking her bosses was a terrible idea. They had the power to break her in ways Peter never had. "Everett…"

"Don't." He lifted a hand, as if telling her not to respond. "I'm not asking you…"

His unfinished statement hung between them.

Yet.

And how could she say yes to him, even if he proposed? Drake would lose his mind, and in his rage, he would destroy everything in his path, including his partnership with Everett. "It's impossible."

"It is." He nodded, but it wasn't in agreement. More like strategic contemplation.

"We can't be having this conversation." Still, her heart was lodged in her throat, strangling her. *Temptation.* Such a seductive, but incredibly dangerous emotion.

She'd have to leave her job. A breakup of their business would have staggering amounts of fallout, financial and otherwise. It would damage Everett in ways she couldn't even imagine. Starting a new business would be a challenge, and Drake wouldn't make it easy.

The repercussions wouldn't end there. Rylee would lose a

man she loved, and he would hate her. That knowledge, living with that, would destroy her.

As if conjured by the tension swirling through the suite, Drake strode in, with energy crackling around him.

He stopped to take in the situation, glancing at Everett and then searing her with his gaze, amber eyes sharp. "Am I interrupting something?"

She shook her head.

Perhaps not believing her, he continued to regard her.

"We were discussing Marcy." Everett cleared his throat. "Post mortem. You're just in time."

Afraid he would see through their lies, Rylee stood. She had to do something to defuse the unsettled feelings crawling through her. "Are you hungry? I can order dinner, and then we can get back to the conversation." She stood and moved toward the house phone.

Drake continued to regard them before finally taking off his jacket. "Yeah." He poured himself a glass of the wine that she and Everett had barely touched.

"The usual?" Steak, rare, with a large salad.

"Thanks."

Then Everett nodded. "Make it two."

She chose pasta for herself—carbs to help her sleep. After the conversation with Everett, she'd need all the help she could get.

When she rejoined the men, they'd been talking for a few minutes, erasing the earlier discomfort. Everett had returned to his seat across from her. Of course, Drake was in his natural place at the head of the table.

"I was waiting to hear Rylee's thoughts on Marcy." Everett turned the conversation back to business, a place they were all comfortable.

Drake picked up his glass. "If you spent two days with her, there had to be something you both saw."

"True." Warming to the discussion, Rylee nodded. "I liked her. She was personable, connected well with others." Including with the owners of all the restaurants they'd popped into. Even though her visits were short and numerous, people showed up, and she managed to shake hands and make people feel as if they mattered. "In that congressional district, she has potential. There will be no incumbent, which is a good thing and a bad thing, right?" Since she knew the answer, she continued without waiting for confirmation. "The field will be wide open, on both sides, which means a primary, which could get nasty. Can she earn the nomination? What gives her an edge? How does she rise above the challengers?"

Though she fell silent, allowing Everett to fill in, he didn't. He just waited for her to go on, allowing her the space to answer her own questions. "She's able to self-fund at least initially. No one else has a campaign bus." With a full wrap, showing her picture—with a bright engaging smile and her arms folded in a no-nonsense way. "Her branding is on point, so she's already hired some talented people."

"Agreed."

"She's smart, has a nice family. Twelve-year marriage, and a social media profile that shows how happy they are together."

"What would you do next?"

For a second, she contemplated her answer. "Hire our own pollster, instead of relying on hers and the ones from the party."

"Well done."

Even Drake tipped his glass in her direction.

"In future I may send you on the trail by yourself."

Stunned, she looked at him. "Seriously?"

"You could do initial vetting. Report back. Especially if we end up signing a national race. I'll be too busy to do much else. And a candidate demands to have at least ninety percent of my attention. For what I charge, that's a fairly reasonable expectation."

All that presupposed that Rylee would continue her employment after the six-month mark. Heart panging a little, she smiled, hoping neither would notice how brittle it was. Working with the two men she loved was becoming more and more difficult. "What were your thoughts?"

"Pretty well the same as yours. I've looked at the potential primary challengers, and I like her early chances. But on the other side, the national party will do anything to hold onto that seat. There could be a candidate we haven't thought of."

That was a chess move ahead of where she was. The opponent on the other side wasn't something she considered. Getting through the primary was critical. But did it matter if Marcy lost in the end to deeper coffers and money flowing in from out of state special interests? "Are you willing to work with her?"

"I'm not dismissing her right away."

But as contemplative as he was, he wasn't saying yes. She admired his thoughtful, controlled way of going through the world. Given what he'd said earlier—about the type of woman he would marry—she appreciated that about him. Instead of blowing up all their lives, he was considering all options. Not that Drake would necessarily behave the same way.

Dinner arrived, and Everett asked Drake for an update on his day.

"It went well." He kept most of the details vague. After all, he'd traveled to Austin on personal business.

From what she'd ascertained, he and Altair were joint investors in certain real estate ventures. If her instincts were correct, that included the building that housed the Retreat.

And because they'd had two days onsite in Austin, she guessed this was a very big deal.

"Altair is scheduled to have a private meeting with the governor next week. Figured you'd like to be invited, Parker."

So Altair was potentially hoping for some incentives on at least part of the deal.

Everett nodded.

"And you, Rylee."

"Seriously?" Despite the fact she wanted to be cool and calm, her wine sloshed, nearly spilling over the rim before she caught herself. After clearing her throat, she grinned. "I'll check my calendar."

Drake responded with a smile of his own. "Yeah. Do that." Then he looked at Everett. "We need a lobbyist."

"How well connected?"

"Top tier."

"That's expensive."

"Make it happen. Within twenty-four hours."

"*Very* expensive." Even as he spoke, Everett reached for his phone.

After dinner, she notified housekeeping that they were finished. Within minutes, someone arrived to clear the dishes and remove the room-service cart. The amenities provided by the Sterling chain were renowned, and she enjoyed the luxuries her bosses demanded when they were on the road.

Struggling to hide a yawn, she said she was heading to her room. She needed to check email, and she wanted to compile her notes from the two days on the campaign trail so that Everett would have them for his files. Even though she wanted to sleep, curling up in bed was probably another hour in the distance.

With the voices of her bosses rumbling in the distance,

she completed her work and then rewarded herself with a bath in the deep soaking tub.

Steam rose from the water as she sank in up to her chin.

Even though she was exhausted, sleep proved elusive.

She tossed and turned, unable to settle. And then she heard raised voices from the shared area of the suite.

The door was too thick for her to make out any of the words, but there was no doubt the debate was heated.

Frowning, she threw back the covers, slipped into a long, silky robe, and then walked into the living room.

Both men looked at her and fell silent. The atmosphere sizzled with the same kind of pressure it had earlier when Drake returned to the suite. "What's the argument about?"

Drake steepled his fingers together. His eyes radiated intensity—reminding her of that first night at the Retreat.

Shivering, she pulled her lapels closer.

"You."

"Me?" Frantically she looked at Everett, praying he hadn't said anything about their private discussion.

"Let me pour you a nightcap." Of course, Everett sought to deflect Drake's attention.

"It's time we cut through the bullshit. Don't you agree?"

Her knees suddenly weak, Rylee sank into an oversize chair. "I'm not sure what you mean."

"I think you do."

"No." She shook her head. But it was a lie. Her pulse careened. She did recognize that look. He wanted her.

God save her. She craved him so much she wasn't sure she could say no.

"I was telling this dick that fraternization is against company policy."

Though she really didn't want the wine Everett offered, she accepted the piece of stemware because it would help occupy her hands.

Drake leveled a look at her. "Is it?"

"There's a copy of the manual on your desk, and one in your email inbox, in addition to the one on the server."

Everett scowled at his partner. "You're an attorney, *our* fucking attorney, and you haven't read something that could be used in a court case against us?"

"Since you're quoting it"—Drake immediately shot back the question—"I assume *you* have read it?"

Everett stood near the fireplace and exhaled. "No."

They both looked at her.

Quietly she admitted the truth, revealing far more than she'd liked to. "It's not in there."

In a way very much unlike his usual behavior, Everett snapped. "It goddamn well should be."

"You each received two drafts asking for input, with deadlines attached. I even set reminders on your calendar." As always, their approach to HR was a disaster, something they maybe hoped would magically take care of itself.

"Drake, I'm damn well warning you—"

"She wrote the manual." His voice was flat, no flash of temper, hard with intent and accuracy. "If she wanted an anti-fraternization policy to be in there, it would be."

The wineglass now precarious in her hand, she set it down on the hearth.

"Of all your stupid ideas, this is the stupidest." Everett's tone was harsh. "By far."

"If you don't want to be part of this…"

"Fucking fuck you." Everett slammed his fist on the mantel.

"That's what I thought. You want her every bit as much as I do." Though Drake continued to speak to Everett, he ensnared her gaze.

Hypnotized, she couldn't look away.

"Our Rylee is a beautiful, intelligent woman."

Passion sparked and flared in his eyes, igniting response in her.

"I will not coerce her." His voice was compelling as he spoke about her. "She can make her own decisions." Now he spoke directly to her. "You have a safe word, Rylee."

She nodded.

"Unless you would like to use it, please come here."

CHAPTER NINE

Torn, Rylee hesitated.

If she accepted his invitation—his command—she would be jumping off a figurative cliff, and there'd be no recovery. Everything would change.

The first night they'd met at the Retreat, she'd given them an ultimatum: the scene was for one night only. It had been an act of self-preservation—one she'd be smart to honor.

Her heart was already in a precarious position. Submitting, maybe having sex, might unravel her already-thin control over her resolve.

Drake extended his hand.

She remained in place. "It has to be all of us, or I can't do this." She'd meant her earlier words to Everett, and she was incapable of hurting or betraying either of them. Just as she wouldn't have Everett without Drake, she wouldn't have Drake without Everett.

"I want you." Everett's voice was hoarse in a way she'd never heard. "You have to realize that. But this has to be your choice."

She nodded. "It is."

"Rylee?" His tone gentler than before, Drake beckoned.

And she was lost in his irresistible allure.

Barefoot, hair mussed, she crossed the room. Then, acting from a place of instinct, not questioning her actions, she yielded to the incredible urge to kneel between them.

"Exactly right." The purr of approval in Drake's voice vanquished her doubts.

She looked up. Drake's eyes were banked with possession. Everett's blazed with passion.

In this moment, she had no doubts. She belonged with them, to them.

With their actions, they both proved it.

Drake fisted his hand into her hair while Everett helped her to stand. "I've had a thought or two about the dining room table."

"Oh?" She tipped her head to the side. While she'd been working, he'd been fantasizing about Dominating her?

"We want you naked, Rylee." Drake was uncompromising. "No modesty this time. We intend to uncover all your secrets."

They didn't want much. Only for her to bare her soul.

"Now, if you please."

Fingers shaking, she loosened the belt around her waist, then she dropped her robe to the floor. In a whoosh of silk, it pooled at her feet.

Closing her eyes, she tugged off her short nightdress.

"Fuck." The sensual intonation could only have come from Everett. "So damn feminine."

When she opened her eyes, both men were taking her in, their gazes approving.

Everett acted first, cradling the sides of her face then angling his mouth across hers for a kiss that was sweet but more powerfully demanding then she expected. He tasted of restrained desire.

Drake moved behind her to stroke her buttocks and trail his fingers down her spine, bringing her alive.

Unconsciously she arched her back.

While Everett continued to plunder her mouth, his hard cock pressing against her, Drake spanked her ass several times—more of a love tap than anything.

Leaving her wanting, Everett ended the kiss.

Drake continued the spanking, harder and harder, making her breathe heavily, forcing her onto her toes while Everett held her gaze and her shoulders, keeping her in place. How were the two of them so in sync that they didn't have to talk?

"Your bottom is turning a pretty shade of pink." Drake traced some of his handiwork. "I think you're about warmed up."

Everett left the room and returned with the paddle he'd bought that first night at the Retreat.

"Never know when our executive assistant might step out of line."

Now that she knew he traveled with it, she might be tempted to sass him or maybe beg for some stress relief.

He sat on one of the dining room chairs and nodded toward his lap.

Conscious of the way her body moved as she walked, she took the position he'd silently asked for. She adjusted herself to be more comfortable. Then she drew a few breaths to settle her nerves as she waited.

Instead of playing with her as she expected, he turned the implement over to Drake. Her mouth dried. No doubt he'd be much more intense than Everett.

Soon she realized she'd underestimated Everett as a Dom.

He lifted a knee, tipping her off balance, lifting her up, forcing her to reach her fingertips toward the floor before trapping her legs between his, ensuring she couldn't get away.

Her butt was higher than it had been, making her cheeks a bigger target for Drake. Had she ever been more miserable?

He gave her a few gentle swats. Already she knew to expect more.

"What's your favorite number?"

Unthinking she responded. "Seven." Then her heart sank as she figured out his evil plan. "I mean three. Three's my favorite."

"Nice try." He laughed. "There's a mirror over there." He pointed. "I want you to watch us own you."

His words shot through her, filling her with desire.

Lifting her head to do as he said was difficult in this position. When she did, her eyes widened. Her breasts, with her nipples hard, gently swayed as she breathed. Her buttocks were already slightly red, and she looked...helpless.

"Start at the top? Or the bottom?"

Which would she be able to tolerate more? "Maybe on my thighs."

In the mirror, his grin was triumphant. "I was asking myself, not you, sweet Rylee."

Everett reached a hand across her back to imprison her more fully when she tried to wriggle forward to escape what was coming.

"Eyes open," Drake reminded her as he caught the middle of her ass cheeks with the paddle.

Rylee's breath whooshed out.

"One." Everett spoke as he used a finger to retrace Drake's mark. "Looks pretty."

Drake didn't follow either pattern that he'd suggested. Instead, he landed the next stroke above her knees.

She cried out, but this time, Everett rubbed her skin, making the tiny pain disappear right away.

"Did you bring nipple clamps?" Everett asked Drake.

"Lightweight ones, like she told us the first night."

This couldn't be happening.

Drake placed the paddle across her buttocks. "It better not fall."

His words might have been conversational, but his command was all Dom.

A few seconds later, Everett shifted. "My knees are getting tired."

"*No!* Please. Don't move." She met his gaze in the mirror. He was freaking grinning. How the hell could she have not realized that Everett was every bit as diabolical as his partner? He wanted the paddle to hit the tile.

Tormenting her mercilessly, he traced his finger up the inside of her thigh, making her twitch. "Everett!"

"Your skin is so soft." He skimmed his touch a tad bit higher, toward her pussy.

It had been months since Drake had held her and given her the sweet release she wanted. She ached to spread her legs but doing so would send the implement flying.

Saving her, Drake returned.

He crouched beside her. "Such beautiful breasts. They've been woefully neglected." He held one in his hand.

Swooning, she closed her eyes.

He tightened his grip almost imperceptibly but released it when it would have become painful.

She whimpered.

"And your nipple...begging for attention." He tugged on it.

"*Noo...*" The pleasure was intense.

"Oh yes." He set the biting clamp.

She jerked, and the paddle wavered.

"Tut-tut." Though he made the comment, Everett didn't attempt to keep her still or move the leather piece to a more secure place.

Together they were deliciously wicked.

Drake flicked the clamp.

Crying out, she tried to stay still.

He fisted her hair and lifted her head to kiss her, leaving her panting.

"I'd say that if you move one more time that thing won't stay where it is."

Helplessly she tightened her muscles, hoping against hope that she could follow his order.

Drake reached farther beneath her to tease her other breast, but since she already wore one clamp, his ministrations were too, too much, and she adjusted herself forward.

Then she froze.

A fraction of a second later, the paddle toppled.

"That was unfortunate," Everett observed.

"Indeed." Unconcerned, Drake attached the second clamp. "Parker, what's your favorite number?"

"Seven. Just like our sweet little sub's."

"And mine is three. So ten more, in addition to Rylee's original strokes."

They were horrible, terrible, mean Dominants. "That's not fair."

Drake tugged on her clamps. "Would you like to argue?"

Frantically she shook her head. "No, Sir."

"Good answer."

He gave her four quick, sharp swats, making the clamps rock back and forth. Then Everett dipped his hand between her legs to tease her clit.

She was so needy she might come undone in seconds.

As if knowing that, they worked together to drive her over the edge.

While Drake paddled her, Everett began to slide a finger deeper into her pussy. If one of them didn't make love to her soon, she'd scream her frustration.

Finally, when it was done, she was trembling, drenched with perspiration from the way Everett aroused her and Drake worked her over.

Drake helped her up. Then Everett turned her to face him so he could remove her clamps. In a way so typical of him— so considerate—he sucked on the compressed tips, restoring circulation and vanquishing the discomfort.

Then he scooped her from the ground and carried her into her room where he placed her on the bed.

Drake followed moments later, tossing a handful of condoms onto the nightstand.

"Uhm…"

"We're going to keep you awake for a while."

Everett undressed first, and she scooted against the headboard at the sight of his enormous, erect cock. The man was a sight to behold. How had she not had any idea how spectacular he was?

"Put a condom on me?"

"My pleasure, Sir." Because her fingers were so shaky, she fumbled with the pack for a few seconds before she managed to rip it open.

He walked closer to the bed, but she slid off the mattress and onto her knees to handle the task.

"We've waited for so damn long."

"Yes." And now she wondered why she'd held out for so long. This was so totally right.

With a growl, Drake strode toward them and somehow managed to lift her up onto the bed. Then he joined her. "I'm going to make damn sure you're ready." He laid down. "Straddle my face."

"Wh…?" The request was so shocking she couldn't even

finish her question. Peter had almost never eaten her pussy, let alone suggested something like that. "Sit on my face, Rylee."

When she didn't immediately comply, Drake looked at Everett who grinned.

He removed a pillow from its covering and then instructed Rylee to place her hands behind her back.

Dazed, she did as ordered. After all, her ass still stung from her earlier failure—although she had been set up for it.

Dick jutting forward demandingly, Everett then moved behind her. "Pull your shoulders together a little more."

Once she had, he worked the pillowcase up her arms. As a bondage device, it was shockingly effective. Because she was trapped, she was helpless against the two muscular, determined Doms with superior strength.

They had her in place in seconds, and Everett took hold of her hips, forcing her down onto Drake's face.

Drowning in mortification, Rylee went rigid.

Until he licked her clit.

Everett grinned at her. "You'll want to fuck his face, lose your inhibitions."

This was so far outside her comfort zone; she wasn't sure she could endure it.

Drake captured her waist and pulled her down a little farther, and then Everett leaned forward to rub her already tormented nipples between his fingers. "He's not going to let you up until you come all over him."

This couldn't be happening.

"Parker, get the paddle. Rylee may need some motivation."

"No!"

"Then do as you're fucking told."

The force in his words galvanized her, and she lowered herself to the position he wanted. Expertly, he laved her pussy, driving her wild.

Everett continued to play with her nipples, tugging, sucking, rolling, even gently abrading them between his tongue and teeth. All the while, Drake's fingers bit into her hipbones, no doubt leaving behind tiny bruises that she'd wear for days.

There were so many sensations—from everywhere—all at the same time, that she could no longer think.

She lost herself in them and the moment, moving her hips, fucking Drake's face as he demanded.

They continued to drive her until she lost her inhibitions. Crying out, she climaxed in his mouth.

Everett looked up. "You did well. Those are the responses we want from you. Pure. Holding nothing back. Your honesty."

After tonight, she would never be the same.

Gently he eased the pillowcase off, and she rotated each shoulder to release the tightness.

Now that they were satisfied that she was ready for them, Everett captured her chin. "I'm going to take you."

Her insides throbbed with an urgent demand. "Yes."

He took the place that Drake had occupied, and she straddled him, lowering herself onto his cock.

"Take your time."

If Drake hadn't prepared her so well, she wasn't certain she could have accommodated Everett.

"Rise up and down, taking a little more each time."

Doing as he suggested, she nodded.

"That's it."

Across the room, Drake tossed his cufflinks onto the dresser, then unbuttoned his shirt. No surprise, but breathtakingly gorgeous, he had six-pack abs. The result of his diet as well as his ridiculous exercise regimen.

Finally she had taken all of Everett, and she exhaled. He held her waist to guide her, ensuring they moved in perfect harmony, rising and falling in the mating dance as old as time.

Drake finished stripping.

His cock was thick and intimidatingly big.

Purposefully he strode to the bed and joined them, kneeling next to her.

"Stroke him." Everett's command was absolute.

Hardly able to think with the way Everett was satisfying her, she reached for Drake. He took her hand and placed it on his shaft, then curled his palm around her wrist and wordlessly showed her what he wanted.

This was…mind-blowing.

She was filled, stretched, following the commands of two Dominants at the same time. "Everett…"

"You're close?"

"I…" She screamed as she came, releasing her grip on Drake as she collapsed onto Everett's chest.

He cradled her against him for a long, long time. Next to her, Drake continued to jack himself off. She'd never seen a man do that, and it was so erotic that her senses swam.

Everett gave her enough time to recover before he started to move again.

Everything about him seemed to be in tune with her, and somehow he managed to stave off his orgasm until she shattered again.

Cursing, he took his release, but the oath sounded more like a prayer. "Rylee… You were everything I dreamed."

Seconds later, she lifted her head from his shoulder to trace his jawbone. "So were you."

Drake's gaze was on her. And though she had lost track of the number of orgasms she'd had, the sight of him in his naked glory was enough to turn her on again.

"Do you need a break, sweet Rylee?"

"No, Sir."

"In that case, I'd like to bend you over the bed."

Everett assisted her into the position Drake suggested. "Your ass is gorgeous, Rylee."

"Made even more beautiful by a spanking," Drake added as he rolled a condom into place. "Red is definitely your color. You'll need to stand on your tiptoes."

With their height difference, even that wasn't enough. She ended up climbing onto the mattress for him to enter her, and then she lowered one leg to the floor.

The position overwhelmed her. He was so deep, and he filled her completely. When she and Everett made love, she'd had some control. Drake allowed her none.

He thrust into her, hard and relentless, a man who wanted his woman to know she'd been claimed.

She was unable to deny him—and didn't want to. The feminine part of her recognized him and the inevitability of her surrender.

He might have been patient over the past few months. But now she knew the truth. He'd been biding his time, playing to win.

"You know it, don't you?"

How did he do that? Read her mind when they were intimately connected? She tossed her head.

"Say it. Admit it."

"Yes! This was supposed to happen." All of it, with the three of them.

"Then fucking come for me. Give me your greatest gift."

Everett dug his hand into her hair, forcing her head back. A mirror hung on the wall, reflecting the three of them back at her. Everett, his dick rock-hard again, possession in his eyes; Drake, his face contoured with the fury of a primal beast; and her, sobbing her surrender as he fucked her hard, then harder.

Having no choice, she gave him everything he demanded.

It wasn't enough.

He kept going until she broke, and he ejaculated, throbbing inside her. Owned as he'd vowed.

CHAPTER TEN

"What is this?" Blinking groggily, Rylee sat up, dragging the sheet with her.

Her two stunningly handsome bosses, dressed in the hotel's robes, pushed through her bedroom door, wheeling a room service cart.

"It's breakfast, in *your* bed." Everett grinned.

Rylee shook her head to clear it.

Her body ached, and she was sore in all the best places.

She and her Dominants had spent the night together, showering, then making love again. At times she drifted off to sleep, snuggled between their strong, sexy bodies.

If she'd gotten more than two hours of rest, she'd be surprised.

Surely they hadn't slept much more than she had. So how did they manage to be so damn bright and chipper?

And ready for more, if the bulges beneath their robes were any indication?

Drake held a large to-go cup of coffee in his hand. "We knew caramel something or other was essential."

All grabby hands, she reached for it. If their intentions

were as wicked as she guessed, she'd need all the sustenance she could gather.

Drake carried the coffee toward her. Even from a couple of feet away, the aroma of sweetness and caffeine assailed her.

"You have to earn it."

With a sigh, she tipped back her head. Did he always have to be such a damn bosshole?

"A thank-you kiss." Holding the cup out of reach, he staked his claim on her mouth, plundering, tasting of mint and seductive demand. He wouldn't simply take what he wanted; he'd ask her to give it.

"That will suffice. For now."

Suffice? It had curled her toes. With a whispered thanks, she accepted the life-sustaining beverage.

"We ordered a lot of different things." Everett pulled a lid off a plate of pastries.

In the middle of the assortment was a chocolate donut, drizzled in frosting and sprinkles. She eyed it, then Drake. "Just one?"

"There were two. In case you weren't willing to share, I already ate one."

Everett plated her treat then offered it to her. Sitting up properly, she smiled her thanks as she accepted.

There was a dizzying array of food. Scrambled eggs, potatoes, fruit, bacon, sausage, even waffles. "It looks as if you had them bring us our own private buffet."

"That's just for you."

"For me?" Were they out of their minds?

The next dish, an omelet and steak, was for Drake. Everett had four eggs, bacon, and a pile of cheesy grits.

Sitting on the end of the bed, Drake lanced her with a purposeful stare. "We arranged for a late checkout."

A task that usually fell to her, the same as ordering food.

And since their flight wasn't until late afternoon, she had an inkling of how they planned to pass the time.

She was astounded by how much food the pair polished off, including some they'd said was reserved for her.

After Everett loaded the cart and wheeled it back into the small kitchen area, he returned to the bedroom and unfastened the belt around his waist.

Her mouth dried at the sight of his glorious cock in full daylight. As he had the night before, he asked her to put the condom in place.

It was a good thing Drake had brought so many.

When she'd done as instructed, Drake pulled off the sheet and grabbed her ankles to tug her to the edge of the bed. "Spread your legs, sweet Rylee."

Knowing not to protest, she swallowed a pang of embarrassment before doing as he said.

She expected him to lick her, but he didn't.

"Open your mouth."

Eyes on him, she complied, and he placed a finger on her tongue. "Suck it."

"Yes, Sir." Keeping her gaze focused on his face, which was shaven despite the ungodly hour of the morning, she sucked and licked, leaving his fingertip wet.

"Good girl."

As always, his words of approval fed her.

Only then did he toy with her, stroking her clit, then easing inside her. At the first touch, she exhaled a shaky breath.

"A little tender?"

"Yes."

"We have lubricant. Unless you'd rather say no?"

"I'm fine. I want this." She looked from one to the other. "Both of you."

"We could try anal."

"Oh hell no." Her reaction had been instinctive and not at all submissive.

Everett chuckled. "You just found something on her limits list."

"It's… I've only tried a couple of times. That was enough to know it wasn't for me."

Drake arched an eyebrow. "Maybe you haven't been with the right partner or been trained properly."

Anal training? That terrified her.

"I'm told it can be rather enjoyable."

Maybe at some future date. If they were still together, something that was far from certain. How would this relationship survive once they were in the real world with its daily demands? All of them had separate paths, and they didn't live together in a fancy hotel where all their needs were catered to.

Drake left her long enough to fetch lube from his bag. Once again, she caught a quick flash of an owl on the side. More than ever she was convinced he was much more than he let on. No doubt the Titans were real, and he was one of them.

She hazarded a glance at Everett. Was he, also?

Drake squeezed a massive dollop of the thick liquid onto two of his fingertips, then waited a few seconds. Maybe to warm it up?

With patience and consideration that she typically didn't expect from him, he eased a finger inside her. He was right about the lube. It soothed the tenderness, allowing her to relax, vanquishing her slight nervousness about playing so vigorously with them again.

Keeping a careful watch over her, he gently finger-fucked her.

Desire took over, and her body responded to his mastery as she moved in rhythm with this timing.

"You're perfect for us."

They guided her into the position they wanted, her riding Everett in reverse-cowgirl style.

Always solicitous, Everett checked on her. "Can you do this?"

The angle was breathtaking, but she loved it. How long would it be until they had the opportunity to play together again?

Since the thought distressed her, she tossed her head as if to banish it. "Yes."

She tipped back her head, and that thrust her breasts out.

Drake climbed onto the bed and knelt next to her, his hard cock angling toward her. Following his unspoken command, she curled her hand around him as best as she could and stroked his length.

Now that they were a little more familiar with each other and she no longer struggled with most of her apprehensions, she gave herself over to the sensation of being taken by one man while pleasuring another.

Everett squeezed and spanked her ass in silent, Dominant encouragement to ride him even harder, faster.

Drake imprisoned one of her breasts, compressing it while tugging on the nipple. She leaned forward a little, so it didn't ache so much, but Everett gripped her hipbones and forcefully drew her back into the position he wanted.

The combination of sensations made her whimper. And Drake smiled. He loved this. And if she was honest, she'd admit she did as well. The pain was enough to feed her arousal but never so much that she was thrown out of the moment. They knew exactly when to push the limits a little to turn her on even more.

"Keep stroking my dick, sweet Rylee."

She'd been so swept away that she'd lost track of what she was doing.

"Need a reminder?" He pinched her other nipple.

Gasping, she lifted herself a little off Everett's dick.

"And one from me?" Everett spanked her ass again.

The way they worked together was awful. In responding to one, she was taken from the other, and both delighted in correcting her behavior.

Suddenly it became too, too much. And she was overcome. "I…" How was it possible that she was ready so quickly?

"Don't come yet." Drake's voice was commanding.

Damn him, that roughness, combined with the way he now growled her name, tipped her past the point of no return.

Crying out, she climaxed, barely able to hold her body upright, panting for breath.

When she was able to stop the world from spinning, she realized Drake was holding her shoulders, supporting her.

"Well, well. Seems you orgasmed without permission."

"It's your fault."

Drake arched a fierce eyebrow, even though a smile tugged at the corners of his enigmatic eyes. "Blaming your Dominant for your failing? Not very submissive-like."

Wrinkling her nose in agitation, she tried again. "It's your fault. *Sir.*"

"Ah. A second mouthful of sass."

She sighed.

"You may want to stop while you're ahead."

Or not.

"And you failed to get me off."

His cock *was* still swollen.

"You also didn't wait for Parker to climax."

Again, not her fault. They'd intentionally ensured her inability to follow their dictates.

"Fetch your paddle, Rylee. You have a lot to answer for."

Frustrating, confounding...*wonderful* men.

After she managed to lift herself off Everett, she scampered from the bed and located the paddle on the dresser, next to the cufflinks Drake had removed the previous night. Something winked in the light. Emeralds? She looked again. That's exactly what they were, and they served as an owl's eyes. Any previous doubts vanished. He was a member of the world's most elite secret society.

"Rylee. Delay will add to your punishment."

"Yes, Sir!" As she grabbed the tool they intended to use for her chastisement, she stalled again.

Her golden heart—the one she lost the first night at the Retreat and thought had disappeared forever—lay carefully nestled between his two cufflinks.

Picking up the chain with its broken hasp, she turned to face Drake. "You've had it the whole time."

He nodded, offering no apology, not that she'd expect one from him. "It's my talisman."

"I'm glad you're keeping it safe."

"Always."

Rylee didn't ask for it back. In its own way, the sweetness of the gesture touched her. She just hoped he treasured her real heart, the one he held in his hands.

After returning the jewelry to the place she'd found it, she carried the paddle to the bed.

The two Doms sat near each other, backs propped against the headboard, and Everett instructed her to lay across their laps. As she'd discovered yesterday, with their muscular legs, that wasn't nearly as comfortable as she'd imagined.

They took turns paddling her, each landing a stripe in a different place on her buttocks and thighs, from a unique angle, and when they paused, one of them—she never had an idea who—fingered her pussy, keeping her on edge.

"That ought to do it." Everett squeezed her burning ass cheeks. "For now."

Drake had to add a caveat. "Think you can behave now, Rylee?"

She was miserable. Now that they'd so totally turned her on, holding back a climax would be more difficult than ever.

"Shall we see?" Drake left the bed to tug her once again toward the edge of the mattress. "Raise your legs straight into the air, please. And then you'll place your knees over my shoulders."

Oh my God. This position would totally expose her to him.

Making it worse, Everett was close to her head, facing away from her. "You're going to suck my dick while he fucks you."

There was no way she was ready for this sensual onslaught.

Yet they gave her no choice.

Sheathed in a condom and taking care to use a generous amount of lubricant, Drake fed his cockhead into her waiting pussy.

She'd never been stretched so wide, so forcefully. How could she possibly endure it?

But the devious Doms had mad skills.

As he worked himself deeper, Drake dampened his thumb and pressed it to her clit, making her shudder. "Now you do it. Play with yourself."

She'd only ever masturbated in privacy. But that was something that no longer existed for her.

"Do as you're told." His eyes held uncompromising ferocity. "Unless you want me to slap your pussy?"

"No, Sir. No." Frantically she shook her head. Her feminine parts were already on fire.

Confusing her mind so that she could no longer think, he

grabbed her hand and placed it where he wanted while Everett spanked her face with his cock.

"You were instructed to suck it."

So many commands at once. Desperate to obey, she opened her mouth and licked a tiny salty drop of precum from the slit of Everett's cock.

That was enough to distract her, and Drake took her completely, leaning forward, pressing his broad shoulders against the backs of her stinging thighs.

As she sucked, they both fucked her, filling her, over-whelming her senses until they all seemed to merge, becoming one.

"Keep moving your hand, sweet Rylee."

Drake's voice was a million miles away, and she wasn't sure whether she did as he said or not.

Then, shouting her name, he came, ejaculating with throbbing, masculine force.

As he stayed where he was, replete, she continued to please Everett.

"Rylee…?"

In response, she doubled her efforts, not stopping until he orgasmed and she lapped up every single drop.

"Fuck…" Everett brushed her hair back from her fore-head, then brushed his finger across her lips. "I'm never letting you go."

She tried to smile and failed. They both knew he could never keep that promise.

Without her being consciously aware of what was happening, Drake eased from her while Everett helped her back on the mattress and to sit up against the headboard.

"Is there more of that coffee left?" she asked while Drake walked into the bathroom. He was such a beautiful, perfect man.

Everett handed her the half-full cup. "We'll order you as many as you want."

"Want? That's for amateurs." She took a grateful sip. "This is an essential need."

Drake returned with a washcloth, and she spread her legs for him. The damp warmth soothed her. Not entirely enough to want to take them both again anytime soon.

They spent the next few hours in a way they never had before, spread out on the bed together, the television turned on, set to a cartoon channel. Totally relaxed, they laughed together, and she rested her head on Drake's shoulder while the amazing Everett rubbed her feet.

It was a moment she wanted to last forever.

And she knew it wouldn't.

Already the clocked ticked away the moments, bringing them closer to the end of their time together and a reality she could no longer deny.

She just hadn't expected it to feel so awful.

❦

Rylee told herself she should be ecstatic. She'd had an amazing time with Drake and Everett. And then landed in Houston. They both had calls to return and busy lives to resume. Everett had tucked her hair behind her ear and thanked her before promising to see her in the morning at work, then headed for his vehicle.

Drake insisted that she ride with him, and Theodore drove to her house while Drake reviewed a file from Altair.

Even before she walked into her tiny, lonely apartment, she was already bereft.

To stave off an emotional crash, she called her mom. After pleasantries were exchanged, her mom feigned an interest in Rylee's life. But she hated politics and didn't want to hear about it. Even while they talked, Rylee heard her mom clanging dishes and throwing in a load of laundry.

After wrapping up the conversation, Rylee called Juliana and received her perky voicemail. At least one of them was enjoying a Sunday afternoon.

Rylee did chores of her own before succumbing to her exhaustion by falling asleep on the couch.

Monday morning, she stopped by the coffee kiosk for her drink as well as ones for the rest of the team. Linda had happily joined in on the morning caffeine kick.

Once Kevin loaded up the tray, he shook his finger as he reminded her to, "Make good choices."

His parting words never failed to make her smile. This time, she wondered how good those choices had been over the weekend.

Her heart rate sped up as she climbed the stairs to the second floor—and it wasn't from the exertion. Instead, she didn't know how to react to seeing her bosses. Or, for that matter, how they'd treat her.

Neither had reached out to her since they'd touched down on the tarmac.

And should she have expected that they would?

Linda arrived, and the designer for the new build called and asked if Rylee could meet at a furnishings store that was going out of business. The man suggested it was a great opportunity to pick up décor at spectacular prices.

Since she was heading out anyway, Rylee grabbed her hardhat.

That week, she rarely saw either Drake or Everett. And when she did, things were stilted, as awkward as she'd feared they be. How was she supposed to pretend she hadn't been spread wide for them, naked, fucked, paddled, restrained?

Late Friday afternoon, both Doms were in the office.

Doms? She shouldn't be thinking of her bosses in that way when she was at work.

Their intimacy in Austin had complicated everything.

From the reception area, Linda called out a cheery good-bye and left for the day. Suddenly oxygen seemed to be sucked from the suite.

"Plans for the evening?" Drake stood in the doorway of Rylee's office, hand in his pocket.

Toying with the heart she'd lost?

Without waiting for an invitation, he entered, dropping into a chair in front of her desk.

Was he suggesting something or merely being polite? "Hadn't thought much past finishing this report."

Everett joined them. "How about we have dinner, and then go back to my place?"

All week, she'd hoped for this. And yet…

Rylee hesitated. Considering the suggestion was madness. Clearly she was more invested in whatever was between them than either of the Doms.

No doubt they enjoyed scening and sex, but it was as if they were able to compartmentalize various areas of their lives. They could fuck and forget. She wasn't wired that way. Perhaps she'd realized that the very first night they'd met.

"Everett has a dungeon."

He did? "You do?"

"We'd like to introduce you to it."

In all the time they'd worked together, neither had invited her to their homes.

She looked from one to the other. They'd worked this out ahead of time? Which meant they had been thinking about her.

Heaven help her. She needed to stop obsessing.

Drake pressed his palms together and studied her over his

fingertips. "I made reservations for three at the Bluewater Bistro. We're hoping you'll join us."

A charming Drake was more than she could resist. The restaurant was highly regarded, one she'd wanted to try. But even at happy hour, with discounted prices, it was a place she couldn't afford.

"Put me out of my misery." Everett chuckled, but there was no lightness in his statement. "I've missed you."

His honesty overwhelmed her objections. "What time?"

Drake checked his watch. "I've already notified Theodore to bring the car around for you and I. Everett has his own vehicle and can meet us there."

"It's kind of early for me to leave work."

"Your bosses appreciate all the extra time you put in." Everett reassured her. "Or do we pay for it?"

"You don't even know if I charge you overtime?"

The two glanced at each other.

Everett spoke first. "Do you?"

"Ask the accountant."

"So you'll go with us?" Drake asked.

As much as she wanted to accept the invitation to ride with him, there were practicalities. "I drove myself today, remember?"

"I'll arrange to have your car delivered to your house."

For every objection, he had an answer.

Rylee stood and grabbed her lightweight sweater and her bag. She'd already made a huge error by sleeping with them last weekend. By going to dinner and Everett's house, she couldn't possibly be making the situation worse.

Right?

CHAPTER ELEVEN

D espite the early hour, the Bluewater Bistro was packed, with people stacked three deep at the bar.

"Good call on getting a reservation." Rylee had to lean closer to Drake to be sure he heard her.

"We had to come earlier than I like, but Myrna was able to accommodate us."

"The owner?" she guessed. Being a Titan seemed to have plenty of perks. One of which was taking care of her vehicle. Before exiting the SUV, he'd asked for her car key, then taken it, handed it to Theodore, and gave the man instructions on what to do.

The menu was filled with Gulf specialties. Surprising her —though maybe it shouldn't—Everett opted for shrimp and grits.

"Sometimes carbs can give you an immediate energy lift." His voice dripped with intent.

Drake chose blackened red snapper with grilled asparagus while she selected one of their numerous salads. From last week's experience, she knew she didn't want anything heavy to eat before they played.

They all skipped alcohol, despite the restaurant having one of most impressive wine lists in the city. It might be nice to return on an evening when they weren't scening.

She picked up her water glass. Once again her mind had spun off on one of its tangents. Being with them in the future was not guaranteed.

Conversation buzzed around them, increasing as more of the after-work crowd arrived. The patrons were mostly young professionals, and no doubt this was a great place to see and be seen or even meet up with someone for the first time.

Everett angled his chair toward her. "Would you like to do the initial vetting of a candidate next weekend?"

"Sure. Where are we going?"

He shook his head. "Not *us*. You."

"You think I'm ready?" She didn't share the same opinion.

"The decision won't be all yours. But I've got a busy week, and I figure you can do the first-round assessment."

"Really?" Excitement zipped through her. Even six months ago, she couldn't imagine being lucky enough to land this job...which made it even more important that she not allow the relationship with Everett and Drake to interfere with her career.

"Wednesday. The event is calendared, so you can find the details. The dossier is on the server."

Not understanding why, she looked to Drake. Maybe for confirmation that he agreed with Everett's assessment?

"You'll do well."

A basket of rolls was delivered to the table, and she broke a piece off one of the yeasty treats, then gave into temptation and slathered it with butter.

Since they were discussing business, she stayed on the topic. "Any updates on Marcy?"

"Our internal polling shows she dropped a couple of points this week."

"Why?"

"A potential challenger has emerged, and he has high likability factors. Of course he could be enjoying a bump from all the buzz surrounding him. But if you were to call central casting and ask for a perfect candidate, he'd fit the bill. Beautiful wife, two small children." He squeezed lime into the mineral water he'd ordered for them all to share. "He's a veteran. Decorated, including a Purple Heart."

She winced on Marcy's behalf. No matter how well qualified a person was or how desperately they wanted the job, there was always a challenger who could snatch away the dream. "So she stands no chance?"

"I didn't say that." Everett glanced at Drake.

"We'll have a look."

With the fact Everett hadn't already dismissed Marcy, it must mean her chances were fairly bright.

"But if he stays in, winning the nomination will be a pricey slugfest."

The food arrived, and the restaurant lived up to its hype.

Rylee was unable to finish her meal. Maybe that was partially from anticipation as they drew closer to leaving.

When the bill was delivered, Drake gave the server his credit card.

She placed her hand on his. "Thank you for dinner."

"Don't thank me. I'm going to take it out of your hide."

With trepidation, she shivered.

The valet brought around Everett's car. Then Theodore pulled up, and she slid into the backseat of the badass SUV next to Drake.

His phone rang. "Altair." He excused himself to answer the call. Even though he was occupied, he placed a hand on her leg, above her knee, his grip tight, ensuring she knew what he was thinking.

When he hung up, he looked at her so hungrily that she instinctively scooted as far away as she could.

When Theodore glided to a halt at a red light, Drake reached to unfasten her safety belt. Then he yanked her across his lap, pulling up her skirt.

She screeched.

"Another reason I like it when you dress like this." He pulled up the hem, exposing her buttocks. "I wouldn't have got one minute of work done today if I'd known you were wearing next to nothing underneath that short thing." He bunched her panties in one hand and yanked hard, lodging the fabric between her labia.

"Drake!"

Without a warmup, he blazed her ass, continuing the harsh strokes until she was whimpering and furiously kicking her legs. Annoying her, she became more and more aroused as each second passed.

Moments later he lifted her and sat her back onto the leather seat beside him, her skirt still hiked up around her waist, her underwear still tight against her throbbing clit.

"That will about cover your portion of the tip. Fasten your belt, Rylee. The light is about to change."

When she didn't comply because she was shell-shocked, he did it for her.

Her mind was still reeling when they arrived in front of Everett's stunning contemporary home with its crisp lines and wraparound banks of windows.

"Wait there." Drake grabbed his toy bag then jogged around to her side of the vehicle to help her out.

Everett greeted them in the grand foyer that revealed the openness of the floorplan.

"This is gorgeous."

"Thank you. The restoration was a challenge, but we were fortunate to find the original blueprints in the attic to use as a guideline. The work took the better part of six months, and I thought we'd never reach completion. But result was worth the disruption."

"I've never seen a house like this."

"It's one of the finest examples of the architect's work." Everett mentioned the name.

"I'm sure I should recognize him."

He shook his head. "Only if you're a fan of this particular style of home."

"I am now." The chrome, the exterior decks with glass panels, the open, curving staircase, and the warm, honeyed woods.

She and Drake followed Everett to the kitchen. It had a lot of original-looking features, but all the modern conveniences that would make it a chef's dream. "This is impressive."

"I'm glad you approve. But we won't be spending our time here. Let's walk over to the pool house."

The backyard was every bit as well-thought-out as the house. The pool was tiled, and a hot tub bubbled invitingly. Numerous palms provided shade for the decking, and potted plants added to the ambiance.

"I'm sure you'll welcome a soak in the hot tub when we're finished with you."

She shot a glance at Drake. "He already started."

Everett grinned. "Your ass is sore?"

"Very much so. Maybe even worse than that."

"Good. That means you're warmed up."

Alone, they were each unrelenting. Teamed up, the men were hellish.

"Take off your clothes."

The order, coming from Everett, shocked her. "Here?

Outside?"

"Does he need to repeat himself?" Drake prompted.

The idea scandalized her. Frantically she looked around. Everett had tremendous privacy. Fences were made of brick, and lush foliage covered them. Some oleanders were at least fifteen feet tall. The nearby houses were single story, meaning no one could possibly have a direct view of her.

"Your rear must not be as sore as you said if you're willing to risk disobeying me."

How had she ever thought he was a kind or gentle Dom?

Her entire body shaking, she unfastened her skirt and slipped it down, tossing it slightly to the side to land on a chair.

"Your panties are exceptionally tight, Rylee."

"Blame your partner for that, as well."

"Blame him?" Everett folded his arms. "He's earned my gratitude. Your cunt is swollen."

The crude word, so shocking, made her throb.

"Are you comfortable?"

"No."

"Good. In that case, leave them in place."

Who are you? Rylee no longer recognized Everett.

She hazarded a glance in Drake's direction. He was grinning as if he was having the time of his life. Not since Sunday afternoon, in front of cartoons, had she seen him so relaxed.

"The shoes are fine also."

No surprise since they too were killing her.

"They make your calves look sexy as hell. Now the top and bra."

After removing them, she tossed them on top of her skirt, leaving her almost nude in front of her Dominants, her fear and arousal a potent combination.

"You're everything I need, Rylee. And more."

Everett melted her heart.

As if by unspoken accord, the men allowed silence to stretch, unbroken only by sounds of nature around them. Then Drake shattered her tension, only to rebuild it higher than it had been. "Put your arms behind your neck, sweet Rylee."

Narrowing her eyes suspiciously she did as he said.

"Ask me to clamp your nipples."

Frantically she shook her head.

"Ask me." Drake's command was ice and steel. "If I have to punish your insolence, I'll make you beg, and then I'll use my clovers instead of the nice alligators you prefer."

Nice alligators?

He captured her breasts. "Ticktock."

She had a safe word, and not for a moment was she tempted to use it, no matter how much she hated this particular demand.

Making her gasp, he sucked on one of her nipples, much harder than he ever had before. Her knees weakened from the shocking feeling.

God, what a horrifying, delicious image. Being naked outside, one Dom watching, the other torturing her.

And when Drake was finished, she did beg for the clovers because they were less painful than what he'd forced her to endure.

"You'd do well to do as you're told."

In the raggedness of his tone, she heard the truth. He didn't want that any more than she did.

Drake crossed to a table and placed his bag on it. He dug the threatened clamps from inside, then returned to her. "I need an assist, Parker."

"Of course."

Suddenly petrified, she looked from one to the other.

"Tug out one of her nipples and hold it for me."

Everett, seeming to relish his part, pinched the barest bit

of flesh between the edges of his thumb and forefinger, the ache exquisite. Then Drake set the clamp much closer to the tip than he ever had before.

Her pussy pulsed, and she did a little dance to distract herself from the awful bite. This was much worse than she imagined.

Together they repeated the process until she was fully clamped.

"How's that?"

"It's the fucking worst."

"Good. You have no idea how much that turns me on."

They seemed to feed on her suffering.

Unable to help herself, she glanced at the front of Drake's trousers. As if demanding completion, his erection strained against the luxurious fabric. Somehow that made the clovers easier to bear.

"You may lower your arms, then lead the way to Everett's dungeon."

So they could watch her ass?

Though she tried, she couldn't walk gingerly enough to prevent the chain from swaying.

"Step it up, sweet Rylee. You wouldn't want me to put a collar around your neck and attach the clamps to it."

She would have shaken her head, but that would lead to greater discomfort.

When she finally reached the door, she stepped aside. Everett keyed in a code, and the lock released.

Once they were sealed in the air-conditioned comfort, he moved to a control panel on the wall to select a lighting mood. Light pink with strobes.

Trying to take it all in, she twirled around. "The place is big enough for play parties."

He nodded. "There's a bathroom in the back if you need it."

In addition to a couch and a couple of chairs, he had a small L-shaped kitchenette to one side. The long wall in the back was filled with hooks, and all sorts of equipment hung from them.

The floor was covered with a type of material that she'd seen in a gym. It was soft and maybe absorbed sound.

Everett had equipped the space with a St. Andrew's cross and several different spanking benches, all covered with padded, hot-pink vinyl.

How many women had they entertained here? Immediately she shoved the thought from her head. It was none of her business, and the answer might break her heart.

Drake placed his bag on the counter in the kitchen area, then returned to her while Everett selected music, loud, drum-and-bass EDM that made the walls vibrate.

Instantly she was thrown into a submissive mindset.

"How are your nipples?" Drake asked, returning to her.

Knowing there was no correct answer, she exhaled. If she admitted she hated them, would he make her wear them longer? If she lied and said she liked them, he'd grin.

So she met his gaze. "I've learned my lesson."

"Have you?" He captured the chain and tugged gently, making her suck in a breath to maintain her balance.

"Yes…" She closed her eyes. "Sir."

"Good." He beckoned Everett to join him.

Simultaneously they freed her. She cried out at the scorching sensation that ripped through her. Each caught one of the compressed tips in his mouth and sucked, laving her until she tipped her head back and the discomfort floated away.

No matter what Drake asked her to endure, his rewards made it worth it.

"We're going to take you places you've never been."

"You already have."

"Sweet, sweet Rylee…" His mouth tasting of approval, Drake kissed her.

Every moment, she fell deeper in love with them.

Everett turned up the music a little more, and the beat pulsed through her, raising her heart rate.

Unlike at the club, they stripped also, creating a more intimate, physical atmosphere. At the sight of their honed muscles and raging erections, her mouth watered.

Drake captured her chin to refocus her attention, and he met her gaze. "Listen to me and do so carefully."

Even if she wanted to, his expression was so compelling she couldn't look away.

"Tonight I'm not asking you for anything. There will be no challenges from me."

She waited for him to go on.

"I will be watching you. But do not push this scene beyond where you want to go. Do you understand?"

They'd battled, and she had a stubborn streak. With his words, Drake sought to protect her from herself. "I do. Sir."

"We want you on the cross. Take off your panties first."

She nodded. When she was naked, except for her shoes, she walked toward the familiar piece of equipment.

Together, they secured her in place.

With her watching his every move, Everett went to the wall and removed two floggers, a small one—probably for her warmup—and a second one that was massive, long and thick, that would cover most of her body, even wrap around her.

A touch of apprehension assailed her.

Drake left her momentarily to return with a U-shaped toy of some sort. "It's a remote-control vibrator. This part"—he pointed—"covers your clit. The other goes inside against your G-spot." He opened his palm and demonstrated the various settings and speeds, from a light, irregular pulse to an enthusiastic and constant buzz.

His movements were somewhat perfunctory as he crouched in front of her, ensuring she was damp before slipping a finger inside to press against her G-spot.

"Sir!"

Then he replaced his finger with one end of the device. He bent the soft silicone, so it snuggled her, and he spread her clit hood to ensure the femininely shaped pad touched her.

He sent a small pulse through the vibrator. In response, she squeezed her butt cheeks.

"How is that?"

"Uhm…" Eyes wide, she finished her explanation. "Yeah. It works."

He grinned. "The fit?"

"Perfect."

Everett began working her over with the smaller flogger, his touch the lightest of dances.

Every so often, Drake turned on the vibrator. Never knowing when to expect it annoyed her. And he never left it on long enough to arouse her.

"How are you doing?" Everett asked against her ear.

"I'm good." Wanting more of everything.

"Ready for the other flogger?"

In his skilled hand? *Yes.*

He used it lightly on her. At least at first. And Drake set the tiny device on a low hum. The silicone pad made tiny, never ceasing circles on her clit while her insides went wild from the unfamiliar shaking against her G-spot.

For a moment the flogging ceased. Then the sound around them was amplified, and the strobe lights flashed brighter and faster. All of it increased her energy.

Everett resumed his rhythmic motions, creating figure eights on her back, buttocks, her legs.

Leather strands bit and thudded in unceasing glory.

Drake turned up the vibrator again, ripping an orgasm from her, so unexpected and so powerful she didn't have time to ask permission.

He didn't seem to care.

On and on they went, and her screams became sobs as she didn't know where one climax ended and the next began.

She surrendered to the moment, to them, allowing her eyes to close and her head to roll to one side.

"You're ours, sweet Rylee."

Impossibly, Drake's sheathed cock pressed against her already-filled pussy. *No!* There wasn't room for him.

"You can do this." He held her still, stroking up, deeper each time, stretching her, driving her wild.

Behind them, Everett continued, but not with the flogger. Instead, he was using something different. A paddle maybe?

The thought vanished before it was fully formed. At this moment there was nothing but them and her heart. They touched every part of her.

"Orgasm with me, Rylee." Drake captured her hair and pulled back her head, devouring her mouth, tongue-fucking her.

On and on it went...until she was lost, floating, fracturing from the inside out.

In her bonds, she went limp, her mind no longer connected to her body.

It was...bliss. Pure, swirling, pink bliss. She smiled, the happiest she'd ever been. And she'd do anything to stay here, forever suspended in magic.

Then...

"Rylee. Open your eyes."

"Uh-uh."

She was snuggled against a man's hard chest, and his heart beat comfortingly beneath her ear.

"Come back to us."

"I'm fine."

Like he had so many times before, Drake dropped a kiss on the top of her head. "I mean it."

This time there was authority in his tone, and she sighed. "Can you go away?"

"Absolutely not."

Slowly she lifted her head. When had it become so heavy? And she opened her eyes.

But it wasn't Drake who held her; it was Everett. And Drake stood in front of them, wearing his trousers and a concerned frown.

She blinked several times. "I'm…" *Confused.* "What happened?"

Everett stroked her hair. "I'd say you reached subspace."

The mystical place she hadn't believed in until now.

Drake uncapped a water and offered it to her.

She managed a sip but nothing more.

"Are you okay?"

More than. "That was amazing." One by one, thoughts flitted through her. How long had she been out? The music was low, soothing jazz. Lights were soft white, and strobes no longer flashed. Somehow they'd managed to unfasten her bonds and carry her across the room. Well, surely they'd done that because she had no recollection of walking. The vibrator had been removed. Even her clothes were on a cushion next to them.

Her entire back side tingled, and a deep satisfaction was nestled in her womb.

"You slept."

If that's what it was.

She took a few breaths as reality sank in, chasing away

the bliss, like the wind blowing a fall leaf from a tree, leaving her disoriented. "Thank you for taking care of me."

"We protect what's ours."

Theirs.

But was she?

Drake had offered no hints about a future. He seemed content to claim her, then go back to his own life until he wanted her again. But every day, in every way, she fell deeper in love, and she wasn't sure how long she could keep doing this.

Slowly she moved, gathering her panties and stepping into them.

"Stay the night," Everett invited.

"I appreciate the invitation." She continued dressing. "But I'd like to be alone."

Drake shook his head. "Stay for a while at least. I want to be sure you're okay."

Because she knew he'd argue until he won, she relented.

Everett and Drake sanitized the equipment and cross. Then they all went to the main house.

"Drink your water." Everett prompted.

She did, letting their conversation wash over her, around her while she sorted through events, trying to put her memory back together.

When what she hoped a suitable amount of time passed, she yawned exaggeratedly. "It's been a long week. Do you mind if I leave now?"

Everett frowned. "I'd rather you not."

She shook her head.

Drake finally responded. "I'll take you home."

In the vehicle, she tipped her head back, drifting off, not to sleep but somewhere on its outer edges.

Being a gentleman, he walked her up to her apartment

and remained with her until she opened the door. "Would you like me to come in?"

"I know you have a million things to do. And I'm going to bed." She raised up onto her toes to give him a quick kiss. "Thank you." With that, she entered her home and locked the door, sealing him out.

In the bath, fragments of the scene returned, but in a disjointed way. It was as if time and space bent when they'd secured her to the cross.

Tonight she'd been more out of control than at any other time in her life. Afterward they'd been there for her, but still, something in her was shattered. She'd stared into the abyss, and now it chillingly looked like her future if she continued to love Drake—a man who'd sworn he would never love again.

Cold despite the warm water, she pulled the plug, then wrapped herself in a fluffy robe.

She was broken, vulnerable, and more scared than she'd ever been. What was she supposed to do with the broken pieces of herself?

CHAPTER TWELVE

Before dinner last night at the Bluewater Bistro, Rylee had told herself that she couldn't have been making the situation with her bosses any worse. After all, she was already in love with them.

She'd been wrong. Things were much, much worse.

Despite the fact she'd soaked in the bathtub after returning home, sleep had remained elusive. The warmth hadn't been able to soothe the aches from their play or from the subspace experience that still captivated her mind. Over and over, she replayed the sensation, flying in a swirling pink vortex. Part of her still seemed to be back there in some altered reality. It haunted her like a dream or nightmare she couldn't shake.

Around midnight, she'd admitted defeat and moved into the living room and curled up on the couch in front of mindless replays of true crime shows she'd seen dozens of times.

At first light, she'd given up the pretense. No matter what she did, thoughts of Drake and Everett haunted her. Frustrated, she brewed a single cup of coffee then dressed in yoga gear and headed for the workout center. Her elliptical training was haphazard at best as she fought off yawns and inertia.

The day promised to be long, and she finally gave in and drove to the coffee shop before going to work. There was always something that needed to be done. And maybe, just maybe, she'd see her bosses. Which might not be a good thing.

After all, she would have no idea how to act, what to say.

To them, they'd shared a scene—one they'd obviously put some prior thought into. But she'd experienced something profound.

For the first time in her life, she didn't feel just alone; she was lonely.

Her mom moving and Rylee catching her boyfriend dry humping one of her friends at a party had been difficult, but not like this.

She took her time, even reorganizing the storage room, before admitting that she was stalling, hoping, waiting...

Annoyed at herself, she grabbed her bag and strode out of the office.

This is why I shouldn't have slept with my damn bosses. Work was no longer the refuge she needed.

She jogged down the steps, and the cloying humidity outside only served to make her mood worse.

The rest of the day, she heard nothing from Drake. Everett sent a text message to check on her. She responded lightly.

His response was all business. *I added the candidate vetting to your schedule. You'll need to be in Dallas on Saturday morning. Take a charter.*

A couple of days ago, his text would have rocketed her to the moon. The words would have meant he trusted her and that she was part of the firm's future.

She wouldn't have been bothered that he hadn't asked to see her, take her on a date.

Something that would have elated her at one time now crushed her.

Late afternoon, all her laundry done, the house clean, her entire next week organized, she forced herself to go out to dinner. Without thinking, she ended up at her and Juliana's favorite tapas restaurant.

Which was another mistake since the Retreat was nearby.

In a few hours, the place would be electrified with excitement and new opportunities. As much as the thought tortured her, she couldn't help but wonder if Drake and Everett would be in attendance.

Rylee's appetite vanished, and she pushed her small plate to the side.

She was wrapped up in a workplace affair, and her integrity would not allow her to be with anyone but them. And heaven knew they were more than enough for her to handle.

Except for the vague discussion with Everett at the Austin hotel, there had been no talk of making anything permanent. Neither Dom was committed to her. Which meant they were free to do whatever they wanted with whomever they wanted.

And she wasn't sure she could live with the constant torment of uncertainty.

As much as she hated it, Peter's awful words were never far away. When she caught him with the other woman, in front of all their friends, he hadn't apologized. He'd shaken his head and sneered. *"You're the kind of woman men fuck, not marry."*

Juliana and Estella—her loyal roommates at the time— had insisted he was full of shit, being hurtful to cover his bad behavior. Rylee would find the right man and live happily ever after.

Now his words were on loop in her mind. Was he right?

Drake—and Everett, she assumed—was a Titan. They moved in a world she'd only seen from the periphery. How much did she truly know about either of them?

With a smile so fragile it threatened to break, she asked the server for a box so she could take her food to go. Then she paid her bill and strode toward her car.

By Sunday morning, she had her answer.

She could not live like this any longer. If her heart weren't involved, maybe. But she'd learned—the most difficult way possible—that she wasn't the type of woman who wanted to have sex without being loved.

And Drake was not capable of offering the one thing she needed.

To save herself, she had to end this.

As exhausted as she was resolved, knowing what needed to be done, even though it was the last thing she wanted, she dressed for the task at hand: a long-sleeve T-shirt, leggings, and tennis shoes. She pulled her hair into a ponytail, then donned a Houston Astros ball cap. Resolved, she drove to work.

Surprising her, the coffee kiosk was open. She needed the sugariness of caramel and the pop of caffeine more today than she ever had.

She made a beeline for the counter. "Didn't expect you to be open."

"Had to turn an order in," Kevin told her. "Do some cleaning, take inventory. Figured I'd try to make a pretty lady happy."

"You did." Maybe the only bright spot in her day.

Whistling, he made her beverage. When he slid it in her

direction, he grinned. "What are you going to do today, Rylee?"

Rip out my own heart? "Work, I guess."

"Nope." He shook his head. "You're going to make good choices."

She smiled. Kevin was always so friendly, reliable. "You got me."

As she took the stairs at a jog, she realized she was going to do just that.

Because it was easier and closer to the industrial size printer, Rylee took a seat at her old desk in the reception area. Linda's desk now. As of tomorrow morning, she'd be running the office by herself. At least she was better prepared than Rylee had been.

After powering up the computer, she updated her resume, her heart breaking after double-checking grammar and spelling. Then, fingers shaking, she sent it to Francesca.

Which meant the only thing left to do was write her resignation letter.

Rylee placed her hands on the keyboard, but the words wouldn't come. Then the computer screen turned blurry. She realized it was from her unshed tears.

Blinking, she forced herself to focus. She needed to go home and heal.

Gentlemen,

The cursor sat there, blinking in mute mockery.

Quickly she googled resignation letters hoping for inspiration. Then she tried again.

It's with regret...

She deleted that. *Regret?* Devastation was more like it.

Professionalism was a cloak she needed to hide behind.

I'd like to inform you...

She hit the delete button. An absolute lie. She didn't like anything about this.

The note had to be short, to the point.

Thank you for the opportunities for professional development. This is to inform you that Friday was my last official day working for K and G and Associates.

The relentless tears now stung her eyes.

I wish the firm well in the future.

Then she paused again.

Sincerely? Regards? Warmly?

Despite her attempts to control them, tears spilled from her eyes and streamed down her cheeks. With the back of her hand, she swiped them away. But her efforts were futile.

Having lost her composure, she pushed back from the desk and headed to the bathroom to give into the sobs that had lodged in her throat.

Get it together, Rylee.

Drake's lovely nickname for her—*sweet Rylee*—played in her mind, bringing another round of tears.

Giving into the bubbling upheaval, she leaned against the wall, arms wrapped around herself but providing no comfort.

Minutes later, spent, she straightened and splashed water on her face. After using a towel to blot the mess she'd made of her mascara, she momentarily removed her ball cap to redo her ponytail.

Then with a shaky exhalation, as composed as she could be, she returned to the reception area.

"What the fuck is this?"

Drake.

Her knees weakened. In his black shirt and tie, wearing a black suit, he was devastating, overwhelming her senses. But fury crackled around him.

In his hand was a damning piece of paper. "Your fucking resume?"

His eyes blazed, turning amber to fire.

"This was nothing more than a steppingstone to you?" Accusation dripped from each word. "You goddamn well used us?"

"No." Frantically she shook her head. It wasn't like that at all. "You're wrong. Please..." What? *Let me explain?* The evidence spoke for itself.

He sat in the chair she'd vacated. After looking at the computer screen, he glanced at her. *"Thank you for the opportunities for professional development?"*

This time, there was no reasoning with Drake. He was feral, and he would go for the jugular.

Holding her gaze, he picked up the phone.

She wanted to flee but couldn't move.

A moment later, he spoke. "It's Griffin. Revoke Rylee D'Angelo's access to the server."

Her stomach plummeted. But what else had she expected?

"Forward her email to mine along with instructions on how to reset the password.

"I would never—"

He slammed the phone down. "Give me your credit card."

Through her hurt and upset, fighting new tears, she grabbed her bag and dug out her wallet. Because her fingers were shaking so hard, it took two attempts to extract the piece of plastic.

She placed it on the desk, then took an awkward step back.

"Your badge?"

Her brain was scrambled, and her thoughts short-circuited.

Then, controlled in a way that was more frightening than anger would have been, he crumpled her resume and threw it at the wall. "You want out, Rylee?" A flash of heat lightning seared his voice. "Then get the fuck out. Unless you'd like me to call security to show you the way?"

Everything they'd had, shared, was destroyed, turned to ashes around them.

Now that she'd had it, she knew what she'd lost.

❦

"What the actual fuck is wrong with you?"

Drake met the stormy turbulence in Parker's gray eyes. After Rylee had left—before he'd thrown her out—Drake had worked out. His fury hadn't diminished. Instead it had become stone-cold hard.

Once he was more controlled, he called Parker and told him to meet at the Braes in the bar—where Drake had been for half an hour, a bottle of fine whiskey in front of him. It was a high-end brand.

He planned to get smashed. And it wouldn't be on cheap shit that would give him a hangover.

Parker dragged a hand through his hair. "You let her go? Without an explanation? After what happened Friday night?"

Parker was much less skeptical than Drake, which made him likeable, but it also meant the man had difficulty discerning the truth. "We'll be fine. We've got Linda."

"We'll be fine? That's all you're thinking about? Business? Jesus Christ. You're seriously fucked up."

Not responding, Drake refilled his glass, then sat back in the leather chair. Thank God it was comfortable. He was going to be there a while.

"Did you ask how she was? What was going on? Give her a chance to explain?" Parker grabbed a glass of his own and filled it. "Aren't you the least bit curious?"

He didn't answer.

"*Especially* after Friday night."

"What the hell does that scene have to do with anything?"

"You didn't call her, did you? Text? Ask how she was?"

He didn't owe Parker any explanations. Drake had been in Altair's lair on the private second floor of the Retreat. Despite what Altair had said in the beginning, the scope of his plans had expanded, necessitating the inclusion of other potential investors. There'd been thirty people in the room, arguing, formulating plans, discussing financing, and the best way to structure the deal—or deals—to mitigate financial risk. Since there had been numerous members of the Zeta Society in attendance—some of whom surprised him —egos flared as each jockeyed for position and defended their point of view. They'd been there the entire day and most of the night. Despite that, only a couple of people had left. And all the time, thoughts of Rylee hadn't been far away. He'd fantasized about going home to her, seeing her smile, pleasing her, then fucking her hard to release his tensions.

"Didn't you notice anything different about her after the scene?" Parker dropped into a chair. "She was shaken. As if the experience had changed her."

"I offered to go inside with her."

"Noble. What a hero."

He dismissed the accusation in his partner's voice. Drake had shown up at the office on purpose earlier, hoping to see her, make her respond to his touch, his kiss. Instead, she'd knifed him in the back.

"She's not Lorraine."

"Hmm."

"Seriously? You really believe Rylee used you?"

The words had been on her computer screen. *Thank you for the opportunities for professional development.*

"That's rich. *You* pursued *her.*"

"A happy coincidence."

"Fuck the hell off with that bullshit. You are a manipulative son of a bitch. Always playing to win. But she was a pawn in your game. I warned you that she wasn't from our world."

The first day he'd seen her, her innocence appealed to him. An act, he now realized. She'd been at the Retreat. And plenty of women attended hoping to meet a man, a Dom. There were other clubs, yet Rylee had chosen that one. Why?

Her heart, his talisman, was now a reminder of his stupidity.

He pulled it out and tossed it onto the small table between them. "Return it to her?"

"Just when I think you couldn't be an even bigger asshole. Put it in the mail. Better yet, be a damn man with some honor and go see her and apologize. At least give her the chance to explain."

Drake scoffed.

"You really are clueless, aren't you? An even bigger fool than I imagined." Though he didn't drink from his glass, Parker picked it up. "She's in love with you."

"Mm."

"You're an idiot. Think about events, about when she changed. She was open to you. Vulnerable. Scared. Trying to save herself." He slammed the glass down. "You know I told her I'd like to marry her."

Rage like he'd never experienced spiked through Drake.

"You know her response? It's always been the three of us. Words she also said before we scened in Austin. Rylee would rather hurt herself than you. And you don't fucking deserve her." Parker's voice also vibrated with harnessed anger. "I thought we could be partners. I was wrong. I'm out."

Parker's words added fuel to Drake's already existing wrath. Coldly he extinguished it. "It'll cost you fifteen million dollars." He knew that number without a doubt. He'd added the rider to their contract. First one to walk away paid.

"That's all it's about to you, isn't it? The money? Winning

and losing? To me, to Rylee, it's about being happy—something you have no clue about. You don't prioritize that."

Happiness? Had he ever experienced it?

"Not everybody uses everybody else."

In Drake's experience, they did.

His father used his mother, then discarded her like yesterday's news. If Drake hadn't sued the bastard, he'd still be denying his own son. Not that they'd ever spoken. Just because it was acknowledged legally, it didn't make the sperm donor into a father. After that day in court, where Jerome hadn't even shown up, Drake had had no contact with the man.

Since he acquired his fortune, plenty of women wanted a piece of Drake. And the one time he'd trusted, Lorraine had betrayed him. He'd never forgotten the scars. Instead he cultivated them until they had locked away his heart for good.

"I warned you at the Retreat that if you damaged Rylee in any way, I would destroy you. You want to play your game with someone who understands the rules?" Parker stood. "You got it. Dick."

He walked away.

For the second time that day, Drake was alone.

He didn't like the feeling. The people he'd come to count on the most were gone. Count on? It was more than that. He cared about them.

He reached for the bottle.

Drake Griffin—ruthless bastard that he was—didn't do feelings.

CHAPTER THIRTEEN

That Everett found Rylee on Monday morning at her favorite coffee shop shocked her. After exercising to exhaustion, then taking a shower, she'd escaped her apartment.

She was drinking her second cup when he walked in and stood next to her table.

"I've been trying to reach you."

On purpose, she'd avoided email. And after fleeing from work, she'd turned off her phone and buried it in a drawer so she wouldn't give into the temptation of calling either Drake or Everett.

"How did you find me?"

"Drake isn't the only one with resources."

"Titans are well connected, evidently."

"So you know?"

"As you said, Drake isn't the only one with resources." Or Google.

Lines were grooved beside his eyes, and for the first time since she'd known him, a shadow shaded his chin, showing he hadn't shaved. He looked terrible, as she no doubt did also.

"May I join you?"

"Anytime." She loved seeing him, no matter how difficult.

He pulled back a chair.

"Obviously you heard."

"He's a dick."

She attempted to smile, but her tummy turned over. It was too soon. So she settled for a small assent. "Yeah."

"I've hired an attorney to dissolve the partnership."

"What?" She shook her head. "This has nothing to do with you. Don't ruin a good thing. You're a kingmaker. The Oracle."

"It'll take some time. Eventually maybe you can come work for me."

That was no more possible than a relationship between them.

"What happened Friday night?"

She'd wondered that herself. "This will sound ridiculous. Subspace…"

He nodded.

"It was like I could see the future."

"Okay." He tipped his head to the side waiting for her to continue.

"It was like floating. But so much more. Colors. Sensations. Being somewhere else." She exhaled, then took a sip while she gathered her thoughts. "Drake's so closed off, and I realized he will never change."

"Playing to win."

"And I love him." She curled her hands around her cup. "I love both of you. And wanting him to give more than he's capable of is pointless, isn't it?"

Everett didn't answer.

"When I was there, I had to confront the truth." And it

had emotionally fractured her. Would she ever again really be whole? "I'll be honest…" She swallowed. "I'm not strong enough to deal with what he was offering."

"He's damaged."

"Aren't we all?" Maybe now that she didn't have as much at stake since her heart was already in tatters, she was able to share her own secrets. "Earlier this year, I caught my boyfriend dry humping a woman at a party."

"Jesus, Rylee."

She shook her head as she exhaled. "And when I confronted him? He was confused as to why I was upset. He was from a wealthy family, and he said I'm the type of woman you fuck."

He winced.

"But not marry. He'd never introduced me to his family, and only a couple of friends. You know, the kind you meet up with at the sports bar."

"You're so much better than that."

"I guess I want to be with the kind of man who is proud to take me to family gatherings, who wants a future." She paused. Until now, she'd been afraid to admit the next part even to herself. "Maybe even a couple of kids."

Violently he shook his head. "I'd marry you in a heartbeat."

"I thank you for that. Under other circumstances…" If Drake wasn't—and always would be—a factor.

Still, she appreciated Everett. His affection had helped her put Peter's hurtful words behind her. They no longer rang true. He'd been an asshole, and she was lucky she didn't invest any more time in their relationship. "I do need a favor though."

"Anything, Rylee. Anything."

"Will you give me a good recommendation? I'm pretty sure Drake won't."

"I'll write a letter today."

Somehow nothing more needed to be said. She'd had no idea that seeing him would be so painful.

"Until we can get our business arrangement undone, I'm not quite sure how we'll manage."

That made her smile. "You'll be fine. Linda is great at what she does. And just so you know, maybe for your new offices, there's an HR manual."

"So you've said."

And if she were to ever write a new one, she'd be sure to add a no fraternization rule. "There's also a set of office policies and procedures. Anyone should be able to sit down with it and know what needs to be done on a typical day. It'll give you a good track to run on with anyone you hire for Kingmaker and Associates."

He didn't smile. Oh how she understood that. Their reason to talk was ending, and the moment was bittersweet.

"What are you going to do?"

"Look for another job. But that trip I had scheduled to New York? I'm moving it up. I need to get away."

He nodded. "Look... I know I'm asking a lot, but I can't lose touch with you. You're too important to me. I want you to be part of my life."

Was a white lie still a lie? "I'd like that."

Then there was nothing else to say.

"Rylee..."

"I'll love you forever, Everett."

"Fuck."

Were those tears in his eyes?

He stood, thrust his hands into his pockets, and then turned and walked away.

For the second time in two days, her heart splintered.

How had her dreams been so close, only to be yanked away?

☞

"Why so morose?"

In Altair's private space, Drake met his friend's gaze.

"You've been here every day for a week. And while I enjoy your company and appreciate you checking out the augmented reality room…"

Where he'd spent countless hours. Anything to escape his own life and its constant reminders of his failures.

Linda was competent, but she didn't provide a sounding board. In short, she wasn't Rylee with her bright, forward-thinking ways.

Truthfully he missed her presence.

Every night when he went home, her absence from his life haunted him. And he fucking didn't want to end the partnership with Parker either—much as that pained him. The man was brilliant, and his closest friend and confidante. Drake had used their escape clause and it's ridiculous $15 million as a weapon. And Parker was willing to walk away from it for some higher purpose.

Drake had won. But at what cost?

His friend—and fellow Dominant. His partnership. His lover. His assistant. His sub.

His heart?

The thing he swore life had ripped from him.

"Morose?" Drake repeated Altair's question, then answered honestly. "Rylee."

Altair nodded.

When Drake had informed the man he'd found her and hired her—despite the fact Altair wouldn't reveal her name— he hadn't betrayed any surprise.

Quickly Ddrake synopsized the last few months.

"And you believe she's cutthroat like Lorraine?"

Drake scowled. That question had been haunting him.

"Do you ever take people at face value?"

"I expect ulterior motives."

"Wise. At times." Altair poured himself a glass of wine. "And where is she working now? A new law firm? A political consulting company?"

To his knowledge, she hadn't found a job. "Point taken."

"Your life; your choices." For a moment, he thoughtfully stared into his glass. "But if letting her go was the right thing, why are you suffering?"

The conversation moved on, and Altair asked Drake's opinion on the augmented reality program he was currently working on. A pair of glasses that could provide the wearer with real time information, calendar notifications, heart rate feedback, even play music. There were limitations, but the possibilities were endless. No wonder Julien Bonds was interested in Altair's work.

Despite the animated conversation, Altair's words returned again and again. *"Why are you suffering?"*

Drake had a dozen other names for his emotional state: anger, righteous indignation, vindication of his belief that everyone used him, recrimination.

But *suffering?*

Didn't that come from love?

The musings unsettling him, he shoved them away. Where he intended they should stay forever.

Despite that resolution, his misgivings refused to remain buried.

It didn't matter how hard he exercised, how many hours he logged at work or in Altair's lab, or how many bottles of whiskey and wine he demolished. At the end of the day, he was still alone with himself and his relentless thoughts.

The next week—one he spent running as far and as fast as he could from his behavior and assumptions—only fueled his demons, ravaging his sleep, destroying his carefully executed plans.

He was punishing himself again beneath the needles of ice-cold water in his shower when truth plowed into him, almost forcing him to his knees.

He'd been a damn bastard to Rylee.

Parker's words at the Braes punched Drake. Rylee loved him.

How?

Why?

He sure as fuck didn't deserve it.

That Altair had essentially agreed with what Parker said —that Rylee was nothing like Lorraine—finally penetrated Drake's skull.

How had he been so blind? So willfully stupid?

He sneered.

Drake was no idiot. He knew—no matter how much he didn't want to admit it. Deep down, he was still the person who was a mistake and didn't deserve his father's love—not even five minutes of the man's time. And when Drake had finally trusted, Lorraine had weaponized his heart. He'd taken both experiences and forged them into armor to protect himself.

Parker was right. Drake was so focused on winning, making life a zero-sum game, that he'd lost track of everything that mattered. He was jaded and guarded. And his feelings for Rylee, ones he'd done everything to deny, had made him doubly wary. It terrified him to admit how much he could be hurt if he opened his heart.

Winning wasn't everything, no matter how much he wanted to believe it was.

And now, in order to win the woman of his heart, he had to be vulnerable enough to risk losing everything.

Rylee, his sweet Rylee, might be Cinderella, and Celeste was right. Drake was no fucking Prince Charming.

He wasn't a man who gave second chances. But now he had no choice but to humble himself and beg for one he didn't deserve.

CHAPTER FOURTEEN

Rylee dragged her suitcase from the trunk of her vehicle.

New York City had been an amazing, vibrant place, and her time with Juliana beyond special, something Rylee's bruised heart had needed.

Despite the sightseeing, the food, the shopping, all the wine, and late-night conversations, Rylee hadn't been herself. Although she was with her bestie, she couldn't shake the unsettled feeling of being all alone in the world. And now, arriving back at her apartment complex reinforced that notion. No one was waiting for her. In fact, other than Juliana who'd dropped Rylee at the airport, no one knew she'd even been on a plane and out of town.

Juggling her bottle of water, her purse, and her luggage, she trudged toward the stairs. How many steps were there again? It seemed like double when lugging this amount of weight.

She hoisted the suitcase off the ground.

"I'll get that."

Looking up, she blinked. "Drake?"

Even though the lighting wasn't spectacular, he was breathtaking in a suit with his hair a total mess and his jaw unshaven—a version of him she didn't recognize. He jogged over to her.

But why?

She'd never expected to see him again.

"What are you doing here?" She shook her head. The answer was obvious.

"Waiting for you."

In the distance she noticed his big, shiny SUV beneath a distant lamppost.

He dug his hands in his pockets. "I'd like to talk to you."

"It's late." And God, letting him get close, even for a minute, was risky. The progress she'd made toward healing—not that it was much—could be undone in seconds.

"Five minutes?"

She closed her eyes, hoping he'd go away. But he didn't. And then he totally stunned her. He took his finger and thumb and made them into the shape of an L and placed them on his forehead.

"If this was a game, I'm the loser."

L? For loser? "What are you talking about?"

"Five minutes?" he repeated.

"Go ahead."

"Inside, if it's okay. I'll take your case up."

While that would be welcome, it would also be stupid. "I can manage."

"I'm sure you can." Keeping a respectful distance between them, he returned his hands to his pockets.

Was her heart still there?

Where had that ridiculous thought come from? Obviously it had never meant anything to him.

"I've had a few realizations. I'd like to share them with you."

She shouldn't care, shouldn't listen. But damn it—damn him—she'd never stopped caring. In the end, she still could deny him nothing.

"Set an alarm. When it goes off, I'll leave."

"I'm not sure I believe that."

"You have my word."

Something he'd never given. "My case is heavy."

"Worried about me?"

All the time.

Rylee walked ahead of him up the stairs. When they reached the landing, she realized she was wearing leggings. Did he even notice?

Because she was so completely unnerved, she stabbed the lock three times before she managed to insert the key.

Moments later, they were inside, her luggage near the bookcases he'd assembled. They were alone, and her pulse sounded in her ears.

"I like the way you decorated."

More small talk? Who was he? And what had he done with her former bosshole?

She moved away from him into the kitchen, needing the physical distance.

But of course, he followed.

He reached for her but then dropped his hand as if honoring what she needed even though he didn't want to.

"Parker knows I'm here. That's the first thing."

What did Everett have to do with anything?

"He's an asshole."

"From what I'm told, it's better than being a dick."

His smile became a wince.

"He told me he proposed to you."

Her insides fell to her toes, and her knees threatened to buckle. "He…what?"

"Twice?"

Not knowing where this was going, whether she could trust Drake or not, she remained silent.

"And you refused." Once more, he waited.

Rylee schooled her features, refusing to confirm or deny anything. She was walking blindly through a potential minefield. Why hadn't Everett given her a heads-up about this? Or maybe he had. She hadn't turned on her phone since her flight left La Guardia. "You know why. Because it had always been the three of us. I can't imagine life without both of you. I won't do that to any of us."

He cracked a short smile. "Everything the asshole has been saying to me is right."

Now that the lighting was better, she saw a tortured gleam in his amber eyes.

"He once said winning was my love language."

Compassion filling her, despite her attempts to keep it away, she slid onto a barstool and waited for him to go on.

"You know about my dad. But Lorraine...? First woman I loved. Turns out she didn't feel the same way."

Ironic. "I know how much that hurts."

"She...used me. She would go to court and watch me in action." He shrugged. With regret? "Of course it fed my ego. She was in the office all the time. Moved in with me. Pillow talk was more about work than our relationship. And when she knew enough, when she got a job at a prestigious firm, she returned my ring."

Rylee winced as she remembered the words she had used in her resignation letter. *Thank you for the opportunities for professional development.*

"Look... I've been a fucking idiot. A bastard to you." His voice was hoarse with honesty, erasing his usual clipped, measured tones. "I cared for you. But... How could I tell you that when I didn't recognize what was happening? I've kept my heart locked away. My father has never spoken to me, the bastard son he's ashamed of. Then Lorraine… It's easier to be a dick than a human who can be hurt."

If she hadn't already been in love with him, she would have fallen right then.

"I'm not asking for sympathy. And that night, when you reached subspace? I knew something had happened. I wanted to stay with you. And I wanted to give you what you seemed to need. Space." He rocked back-and-forth on his heels. "I misread you, and I'm sorry." His words were real, heartfelt, coming from deep inside him.

She slid from her barstool but grabbed the back for stability.

"I was told in no uncertain terms that I was no Prince Charming. Well, the exact words were no fucking Prince Charming."

"Everett?"

"No. Someone else. A Titan who I hope you will meet."

She tightened her grip. He was speaking in terms of a future. Or was it her desperate imagination?

"In the last few days, I've faced some awful truths about myself. I've made it a habit not to give people second chances. Yet here I am to beg you for one. And goddamn it, Rylee, I know I don't deserve it."

"Drake, I…" She swallowed her tears. His words touched her. But if she agreed, would they be right back in the same place they'd been when she resigned?

"I love you, Rylee."

Her knees buckled. And he was there, catching her, pressing her close, placing the gentlest of kisses on her forehead. How was this possible?

"What I'm trying to say is this… I want to spend the rest of my life with you. And the fucking annoying Parker."

She wiggled back to look up at him. "I can't… I don't…" Her mind reeled.

"I want to propose."

"You know I can't accept." Her voice cracked. "I love you with my entire heart, but I love Everett too." Her hopes had soared only to plummet.

"That may be what I adore most about you. Your sense of fair play, your integrity. He predicted you'd say that if I asked. I hate that he's right so often."

She smiled.

"So I'll wait for sixty seconds."

"Sixty seconds?" She laughed.

He pulled out his phone and shot off a text message. "Fifty seconds. More or less."

A knock sounded on the door.

"Even faster than I expected."

Still not able to take this in, she answered the summons.

Everett—tie loose, jacket unbuttoned—stood there. "Since you allowed that dick in, I assume I'll get an invitation?"

Tears, this time happy ones of joy, flooded her eyes. "Yes. Yes."

He kissed her madly, passionately, in a now-and-forever way.

With deep, threatening meaning, Drake cleared his throat.

She and Everett parted, then, holding hands, walked to Drake.

Taking her other hand, he lowered himself to one knee. Her pulse fluttered as he reached into an interior pocket in his suit coat.

She looked at him, then Everett who squeezed her hand reassuringly.

Drake went first. "I love you, Rylee."

Then Everett took a turn. "I love you, Rylee." Then he lowered himself to one knee.

This was more than she dared dream. A happily ever after she thought was for others and not her.

"Rylee D'Angelo." Everett and Drake spoke together. "Will you marry us?"

Shaking, tears fell.

She couldn't talk through the swells of happiness.

"Is that a yes?" Everett asked.

Still unable to find her voice, she nodded.

Drake slid a ring onto her finger. The diamond was brilliant, like their love.

They stood, and she took turns kissing them both, celebrating their lives together.

"Dare I hope you have a bottle of champagne?" Drake asked. "Or wine?"

She laughed. "The most exquisite cardboard-aux."

Both men groaned.

Drake looked at Everett. "I'll ask Theodore if he minds making a run to the liquor store."

"We have a couple more things to talk about." Drake was back to business. The changes he wanted to make would take time.

"We want you to come back to K and G and Associates. Linda has threatened to quit if you don't."

"Does this have anything to do with your proposal?"

Both frantically shook their heads. "I'll want a raise. And to be back on track for my six-month bonus."

Drake shook his head and looked at Everett. "Who taught this woman to negotiate?"

She answered the question herself. "I learned from the best."

"And I still need you to vet the candidate in Dallas."

She shook her head. "Anything else?"

Again the men exchanged glances.

"The project manager on the new offices quit."

Everett exhaled a whistle. "Even I didn't know that."

"Seems I'm difficult to work with."

Everett shrugged. "Who could have guessed?"

"Anything else?" she asked one more time.

"Yeah." Drake hesitated, then cleared his throat.

He reached into his jacket pocket one more time and pulled out a heart choker. It was unbelievably similar to her original one, but it was bigger and no doubt crafted from real gold, and it had an actual lock on it.

"Parker and I both have keys."

His action had touched her very soul.

"Will you wear it?"

"Be our submissive?" Everett added.

There was nothing she wanted more. She looked at Drake. "Yes, Sir." Then at her other Dom. "Yes, Everett. I love you both. I commit myself to you. I submit to you. Collar me."

They did, each keeping a key.

The two had made her whole, and she couldn't be happier.

Everett swept her from her feet and followed Drake into her bedroom where they claimed her for life.

EPILOGUE

"Did you like the food?" Rylee asked, looking at her Doms.

Because it was her favorite, they'd agreed to have dinner with her at the tapas restaurant. They'd ordered one of everything.

"It was great." Drake nodded. "When's dinner?"

She frowned. "You could have ordered an actual meal."

"Or we can go out again after our meeting with Altair."

Even after being in a committed relationship for four months, she sometimes didn't know whether he was serious.

"He's serious." Everett shrugged. "As for me, I liked the food, and I'm full. I'm glad you suggested it."

The server brought the bill, and Drake paid, even though she now could have. As part of the complicated legalities involved in getting married, both men had signed agreements, guaranteeing her incredible wealth. And they'd opened an account in her name and made a staggering deposit to it. They insisted they wanted her to be an equal, not just an employee.

If this was a dream, she never wanted to wake up.

Once they left the restaurant, they were heading to the Retreat but not to scene. Nerves and excitement careened through her, knowing she was going to meet the mysterious Altair in his private space.

She'd learned that Drake was one of the mystery investors in the physical building. Altair did own the club, and he paid rent to the corporation for his use of the space.

Tonight there would be other potential investors, and Altair hoped becoming acquainted with Drake, Everett, and Rylee might entice them to stop stalling and sign on the dotted line.

Every moment with Everett and Drake was an adventure.

Within days of her return from New York City, she and Drake had moved into Everett's spectacular house—a place that now needed more remodeling. They all agreed the bedroom they shared needed to be larger. And since Drake was a fashion fanatic, a larger closet was a must. Rylee had to admit she would enjoy a soaker tub as well. Her ass was often sore, and baths with Epsom salts had become a necessity rather than a luxury.

The new offices were almost done, not a minute too soon. Linda had needed to hire a part-time assistant. Her desk was in the reception area, and a pollster was often holed up in the conference room. K and G and Associates was growing.

Last week Rylee and her fiancés had set a date for their wedding. As far as anyone knew, she was marrying Drake. Beforehand, they would have a private commitment ceremony, and there was no doubt that, for her, it was the three of them forever.

But the decision to have a formal gathering added to their chaos and stress level. To offload some of that, Francesca had recommended a wedding planner. Rylee liked Mrs. Henderson immediately and hired her on the spot.

Drake had been more guarded. While he didn't object to

the planner herself, she was the mother-in-law of Jaxon Mills, the controversial podcaster who couldn't seem to keep himself out of the news. Drake wanted assurances that Mrs. Henderson wouldn't add her obnoxious son-in-law to the guest list. Rylee wouldn't promise that. Willow, the man's wife, was reportedly lovely. And since Mills was a Titan, he might expect to attend.

Rylee suspected it wouldn't be the first objection Drake raised on their long road to matrimony.

"Ready?" Drake stood, then pulled back her chair. But instead of stepping back, he leaned forward, making her jump. Instinctively she touched her choker as he whispered in her ear. "Are you wearing underwear?"

How could he still manage to scandalize her? "No, Sir."

"Correct answer, sweet Rylee."

Everett offered his arm.

Outside at the curb, Theodore opened the door of the new, larger vehicle. Since there were now often three passengers in the SUV, Drake wanted transportation with seats that faced each other. A badass, four-wheel drive version of a limo. Besides, he'd added, what if they needed room for car seats?

They arrived at the Retreat in mere minutes. Though it was Tuesday, Miss Watson was on duty behind the desk.

"Do we need to sign in?"

Drake shook his head. "Buzz us through?" he asked after greeting the woman.

"Of course, Sir."

Drake guided Rylee past some potted palms and then stunningly through a panel on the wall. "This is like Wonderland."

Everett nodded. "Couldn't agree more."

They emerged from an elevator on the second floor into a wide-open space with modern art on the walls, comfortable chairs, a bar, and what looked to be a superb buffet on a long, narrow table.

"Thank God," Drake said.

Moments later Altair joined them. The men shook hands. Then he turned his commanding presence to her.

"The lovely…"

Her Doms looked to her to provide an answer. Scene name or legal one? Why had they not thought to discuss this ahead of time? "Uhm…" Then she cleared her throat and pulled back her shoulders. "Rylee D'Angelo, Your Grace."

Like Drake had done that first night, Altair raised her hand to his lips.

Drake's scowl was fast, a return to the feral nature she hadn't seen in months. Everett placed a warning hand on his partner's shoulder.

"My pleasure, Rylee. Having met you formally, I understand why neither Everett nor Drake ever returned to the Retreat."

Her heart skipped over its next beat.

"And in my quarters, unless you're my submissive—"

"Which she damn well isn't." Drake's amber eyes flashed.

She frowned. What was wrong with him? She'd never seen this side of him before. No longer just a bosshole, but an alphahole as well.

"No implication otherwise." Altair shot his friend a smile. "I don't stand on ceremony in my private quarters. Call me Altair, please."

"I'm afraid I might mess up…Altair."

"You'll be forgiven."

At the very least, he was a man she instinctively wanted to address as *Sir*.

"Come. I'd like to introduce you to some of my associates. Wine? Whiskey?" He signaled to a server.

"Save the respectful titles for the bedroom, sweet Rylee. Otherwise you'll get the paddling of your life tonight."

Drake could only be soothed in one way. She smiled. "As far as I'm concerned, Sir, there are only two Doms on the planet."

He trailed his fingertips down her spine in a possessive but seductive way. "You know how to soothe the beast."

As they walked, she took his hand and traced a heart on his palm.

Everett grinned at her. "You could teach a class on Dominant temper management. Maybe I'll suggest it to Miss Watson."

When they reached the other guests, Altair performed the introductions. "Daniel and Noah Armstrong."

Unable to help herself she looked from one man to the other. They were gorgeous and identical twins.

"And their bride, Kristin."

Their bride?

Altair's guest list decision had been rather strategic.

Everyone shook hands, and Rylee hoped she had an opportunity to speak with Kristin in private. She could use advice from someone who knew what she was dealing with.

A server took their drink order and returned quickly. And since they all had so much in common, conversation flowed easily.

About ten minutes later, the elevator dinged again.

Their host excused himself to greet them, ensure their drink order was taken, then performed another round of introductions. "Ethan Slater. A member of our fine military."

She gave him a warm smile as she shook his hand. "Thank you for your service."

"Doing my job, ma'am."

Didn't heroes always say that?

"And Cormac Flanagan."

"An Irish background, I assume?"

"Aye."

Altair certainly knew some charming gentlemen.

As the evening progressed, more people arrived, a dizzying array of names. Though Drake had prepped her in advance, she couldn't keep them all straight. Rafe Sterling and his wife, Hope. The surname she recognized because of the memorable stay with her Doms in one of his Austin hotels. Others she hadn't committed to memory. Elizabeth and Braden Gallagher. Grant Kingston who worked for the genius, Julien Bonds.

By the end of the evening, despite a glass of wine, she was able to attach names to faces, something she'd need to be able to do easily as a Titans hostess.

Her new life would not be boring.

Rylee was still having fun chatting when Drake found her. "I'm ready to take you home. Parker and I are done sharing you with the rest of the world. Seeing you in action has made me hard."

She blinked. "Well, of course, Sir."

Once they were inside the foyer of their home, he stripped the dress from her, not waiting for her to do it herself.

Fuck. No bra either?"

"Must have forgotten, Sir."

"I don't know how you get more beautiful every day."

"Upstairs, Rylee." Everett's voice was just as ragged as Drake's. "We want you."

Exaggerating her movements, she allowed her hips to sway from side to side and did as he instructed. Once inside the room, she stopped, turned, and then sank to her knees, aware of her tiny heart dangling from her choker.

"You know this is a forever thing, right?" Drake demanded. "You're ours to love."

"Yes, Sirs." Drake might not be Prince Charming, and she might not be Cinderella, and Everett hadn't quite been restored to his kingmaker throne, but it seemed her fairytale life had a double-dose of a forever-after, happy ending.

Smiling, she waited on their next command.

◊ ◊ ◊ ◊ ◊

Thank you for reading Theirs to Love. Drake was one of those heroes who consumed me. The writing was a whirlwind from beginning to end. And Everett? Swoon. Such a heavenly Dom. To be sure, he can be demanding, but he wraps it in tenderness. He's so different than Drake, and together, they're magic.

Be sure to read the next delicious Titans ménage story, *Theirs to Wed*

An officer. A gentleman. And they intend to claim her forever.

Temporarily marry a billionaire for cash? Amelia Ryan would never consider such an appalling idea…except her grandmother needs care Amelia can't afford. Cormac Flanagan is gorgeous and powerful. But he's also half of the Dastardly Duo, who, along with his heroic cousin Ethan Slater, are notorious for breaking hearts all over Texas.

Still, when Cormac offers Amelia a million dollars for her hand, he insists she'll be his bride—but his and Ethan's wife—in all ways. Once she's theirs and surrenders to their seductive touch, how will she ever protect her heart from the sensual, devastating Dominants?

DISCOVER THEIRS TO WED

Don't miss out! VIP newsletter subscribers receive special bonus reads—epilogues, deleted scenes, and more. Of course, you'll get all the Scandalicious news about upcoming releases, special promotions, and sales.

Become a VIP newsletter subscriber today!

If you like two protective, sexy, dominant alpha males, a steamy touch of BDSM, some great suspense, and a heart-wrenching second chance at love, I invite you to read Come to Me, a BDSM romantic suspense novel.

There's a cool million-dollar bounty on the head of Hawkeye commander Wolf Stone. Nate and Kayla will do anything to protect him, but will the cost to their hearts destroy them....?

★★★★★ Ménage, BDSM, Sierra Cartwright...YES PLEASE! ~Amazon Reviewer

DISCOVER COME TO ME

Turn the page for an exciting excerpt from COME TO ME

COME TO ME

CHAPTER ONE

HAWKEYE

S *hit.*

Nate Davidson opened his eyes and tried to shake away the stars that had exploded in his head and stolen his vision. It took several tries before the image of strong, tall, dark, and dangerous Wolf Stone blinked into focus. And when it did, Nate was certain he'd never seen anything better.

It'd been a long time. Too damn long.

"You're lucky I didn't tear your fool head off."

Nate flexed his jaw to make sure it still worked. "Feels to me like you did."

"What the fuck are you doing here?" Stone's voice was deep and ragged, cut glass on velvet.

"You're not glad to see me? I thought you'd start looking for a fattened calf." Nate knew what real danger was. It had nothing to do with his battered body or the nasty storm snarling its way over the Rocky Mountains. Danger was Wolf Stone. And Nate was in the bigger, stronger man's sights.

Nate struggled to get his elbows behind him. Damn mountains were made of rock, not the best pillow under any circumstances. Downright painful when you'd had your clock cleaned by a tank of a man. "Mind if I sit up?"

"Stay where you are."

Lying on the ground, looking well over six feet up into Stone's cold blue eyes left Nate at a disadvantage—or, rather, at a greater disadvantage than he usually was around Stone. "Hospitable as always, aren't you, boss?"

"All trespassers get the same treatment."

No matter how hard either of them tried to pretend otherwise, they both knew Nate was no ordinary trespasser.

And Stone was no ordinary property owner.

He'd commanded several missions that Nate had been assigned to. Every person selected had to meet rigorous physical standards. By any measure, Nate was a good-size man, an inch over six feet, two hundred seven pounds of lean muscle.

Still, Stone had him by two inches and at least twenty pounds. Even now, recouping from injuries, Stone had effortlessly brought Nate down. Well, that was an understatement. Stone had tossed Nate like an old magazine.

"Still waiting for an answer to my question, Davidson."

Sometimes, only the truth would do. "When you refused protection, Hawkeye sent me."

"You're here," Stone demanded incredulously, "to protect *me*?" He raised a dark eyebrow in a way that made grown men cower. Nate had seen it happen, and he refused to admit to himself that it made him cower as well.

"Who'd have imagined?" *Ludicrous.*

Stone sheathed his knife. The weapon was overkill. He only needed his hands in order to tear a strip out of someone's hide.

"Tell Hawkeye I said thanks, but no thanks. You can find your own way off the ranch." Stone turned.

If he hadn't been looking for it, Nate might not have noticed Stone's slight limp. *Stubborn man.* The threat against his life was real and imminent. He was the only eyewitness to the hit that had taken out Elliott and Lisa Mulgrew. Word on the street was that some lucky bastard would get a cool million dollars if Stone didn't make it to court to testify against Michael Huffman, the murderer.

While Stone was holed up in his fortress, he was safe enough. But once he left Cold Creek Ranch, he'd need the backup.

"So," Nate called out when Stone got about ten paces away, "you're not interested in knowing how I breached the perimeter?"

"You got exactly nowhere before your ass was mine." He continued on without looking back.

"Storm's brewing, man!"

"You'll get wet."

Well, hell. Nate collapsed back onto the unforgiving ground. That'd gone well.

Stone disappeared over a ridge, vanishing into thick Ponderosa pines.

In a nearby tree, a hairy woodpecker—nasty little bastard —beat out a staccato that matched the throbbing headache in Nate's temples.

Under any circumstances, he deferred to Stone. The man exuded a palpable loyalty-inspiring authority. Even now, when Stone didn't want assistance, didn't want to be protected, Nate had no intention of leaving. Stone was as determined as the mountains were rugged. Then again, so was Nate.

Hawkeye hadn't recruited Nate for this job. He, plus the

helicopter pilot and copilot, had volunteered. It had taken days of planning, and he refused to admit failure.

Half a dozen raindrops pelted his cheeks.

Even in the past few minutes, the storm had gathered clouds and whipped them together with wind to descend the eastern slope of the Continental Divide.

Could this get any worse?

Lightning slashed through the swollen gray sky, igniting a path of cloud-to-cloud strikes.

Yeah. It had gotten worse.

~~*~~

Wolf Stone, no matter how drop-dead gorgeous he was, was out of his freaking mind. And an asshole to boot. "You left Nate out there?" Kayla Fagan demanded. "Have you seen the weather?"

"He's not made of sugar."

"Meaning he won't melt?"

"Exactly."

"If this is how you treat your fellow operatives, what do you do to your enemies?"

He shrugged. "None of them left alive to tell." He smiled, and it did nothing to soften his features. The quick curve was more wicked than anything, making his eyes darken, reminding her of those few moments of twilight before the sky devoured the sun.

He strode from the kitchen, and she followed. "Mr. Stone—"

"Wolf, or just Stone." He didn't slow down. "And I'm not worried about how I'll sleep tonight." He crouched in front of the hearth, tossing kindling into the empty fireplace grate.

When she first heard he was holing up in a log house on a ranch, she'd pictured a remote, barely inhabitable two-room cabin.

She couldn't have been more wrong.

Wolf Stone enjoyed luxury, and his home was the intersection of comfort and high-tech. This room, more than any other, gave a nod to his heritage. A rug, painstakingly woven by his grandmother, hung from one of the walls. Another rug, not crafted by his family, dominated the area near the fireplace.

In other rooms, he flicked a switch to ignite the gas fireplaces, but in this one, he obviously preferred to build it himself.

Even though she was stunned by his bad behavior, she couldn't help her fascination as she watched him. His shoulders were impossibly broad. Long black hair, as wild as he was, was cinched back with a thin strip of leather. And Lord, he had the hottest ass she'd ever seen, and a cock with plenty of potential.

Not that she'd actually seen it full-length.

But at night, when he thought she was asleep, he walked around the house in the buff.

Last night, his dick had been partially erect, and the darkened view had inspired her dreams and nearly made her forget her job.

Lucky for her, at least part of the time, she was required to have her hands on him. She just hadn't quite figured out how to professionally get him to take off all his clothes to touch his naked body.

Thunder cracked, and she worried about Nate. "I think you should at least invite him in until the storm passes." Even though it was summer, weather could be extreme at this elevation.

"You going to nag me?"

"Convince you to change your mind, using my excellent powers of verbal persuasion."

"Save your breath. Hawkeye doesn't need to squander its resources on me."

Hawkeye Security. The company they all worked for was named after the man who'd founded it, a man she, and most others, had never met. Wolf, she'd heard, was one of his closest advisors.

With their highly trained men and women, Hawkeye provided world-renowned protection. They recruited former Special Forces operators, ex-cops, bodyguards, lots of IT people, and other brainiacs, including some who worked remotely out of small, private offices. The higher the stakes, the likelier it was that Hawkeye would be the firm of choice.

Her teammates were the best in the world. She was proud to be one of them. "Hawkeye brought me in as well," she reminded him. "Maybe he would go to these extraordinary lengths for any one of us, but maybe he wouldn't. All I can say is he obviously considers you important."

Stone struck a match, filling the room with the sharpness of sulfur. "My mind is made up."

"But—"

"I told Hawkeye not to send anyone. I meant it."

"You can have a heart, just until the weather clears. Then you can go back to your regularly scheduled…" She stopped short of saying assholeishness. "Grumpiness."

His mouth was set, brooking no argument. "Let it be."

Huge splatters of rain hit the floor-to-ceiling windowpanes.

Wolf might be able to sleep at night if he left his comrade out there, but she would toss and turn with worry.

Decision made, Kayla crossed to the hallway closet, pulled open the gigantic golden oak doors, and took out a raincoat. She also grabbed her gun and checked it before tucking it into her waistband. She snatched up a pair of compact binoculars and a compass and was shoving her arms in the sleeves of the yellow slicker as she walked through the great room on the way to the back door.

"What do you think you're doing?"

"Exactly what you said. I'm saving my breath." Kayla spared him a glance. "I decided not to argue with you."

"Stop right there."

He spoke softly, but his voice snapped with whiplash force. Despite herself, she froze. She'd faced untold danger, but this man, unarmed, unnerved her. A funny little knot formed in the pit of her stomach.

Kindling crackled as fire gnawed its edges.

"Turn around." His voice was terrifying in its quietness. "Look at me, Fagan."

Struggling not to show the way she was trembling, she turned.

He stood. "I will be very clear, Ms. Fagan. You are here at my pleasure." He took a single step toward her. "I will not be disobeyed."

His statement was loaded with threat.

Wildly she thought of the room in the basement, the one with crops and paddles hanging from the walls. The one she'd been forbidden to enter, and the door she'd opened the first time he'd left the house.

She locked her knees so she didn't waver. "I've never been much for obedience."

"Nathaniel Davidson is far from helpless."

"He's a fellow member of Hawkeye. I'm not allowed to leave him out there. And I won't." She met his gaze and ignored the fury blazing there. "Really, Mr. Stone, I don't care if it gets me fired." *Or worse.* She pivoted and walked away.

The wind whipped at the door, nearly snatching it from her hand.

She turned up the collar of her ineffective raincoat. There was never anything friendly about a Rocky Mountain storm.

She'd grown up in Tucson where torrential rains were common during the monsoon season. They cooled the weather to bearable seventy-degree temperatures, but this— it was freaking like winter.

Fortunately, she didn't have far to trudge. From her conversations with headquarters, she had a pretty good idea of where the insertion was supposed to happen. And in less than fifteen minutes, the ground beneath her sizzling with electrical ferociousness, she saw a streak of orange.

She grinned.

Members of her team were smart. Nate had donned a reflective safety vest. That would, at least, stop friendly fire.

"Davidson!" When she got no response, she called out a second time.

He started toward her. "Come to rescue me, have you?" he shouted above the roar of the wind. "Bet Stone told you to come."

"He sends his regards and invites you to sit next to the fire while he pours you a cognac."

Nate laughed. "How much trouble are you in for coming after me?"

"He didn't threaten to flay the skin from my hide."

"Doesn't mean he won't."

"Thanks. That's a comforting thought."

"He doesn't know?"

"Who I am? No." She shook her head. "He thinks Hawkeye sent him a physical therapist."

Nate grinned. "Do you know enough about that to do no harm, doc?"

"Uh… I watched a special on the internet."

Thunder crashed.

"I ought to write both of you up."

Wolf. Her breath threatened to choke her. How much had he overheard? It shouldn't have surprised her that he'd followed, that he'd effortlessly covered the same ground she had in far less time. The man was in shape, and he kept himself sharp.

Over the lash of the summer storm, his voice laden with command, he said, "Both of you, back to the house. Now."

ABOUT THE AUTHOR

I invite you to be the very first to know all the news by subscribing to my very special **VIP Reader newsletter**! You'll find exclusive excerpts, bonus reads, and insider information.

For tons of fun and to join with other awesome people like you, join my Facebook reader group: **Sierra's Super Stars**.

And for a current booklist, please visit my **website**.

USA Today bestselling author Sierra Cartwright was born in England, and she spent her early childhood traipsing through castles and dreaming of happily-ever afters. She has two wonderful kids and four amazing grand-kitties. She now calls Galveston, Texas home and loves to connect with her readers. Please do drop her a note.

ALSO BY SIERRA CARTWRIGHT

Titans
Sexiest Billionaire

Billionaire's Matchmaker

Billionaire's Christmas

Determined Billionaire

Scandalous Billionaire

Ruthless Billionaire

Titans Quarter
His to Claim

His to Love

His to Cherish

Titans Quarter Holidays
His Christmas Gift

His Christmas Wish

His Christmas Wife

Titans Sin City
Hard Hand

Slow Burn

All-In

Titans: Reserve
Tease Me

Titans Captivated

Theirs to Hold

Theirs to Love

Theirs to Wed

Theirs to Treasure

Hawkeye

Come to Me

Trust in Me

Meant For Me

Hold On To Me

Believe in Me

Hawkeye: Denver

Initiation

Determination

Temptation

Bonds

Crave

Claim

Command

Donovan Dynasty

Bind

Brand

Boss

Mastered

With This Collar

On His Terms

Over The Line

In His Cuffs

For The Sub

In The Den

Collections

Titans Series

Titans Billionaires: Firsts

Titans Billionaires: Volume 1

Billionaires' Quarter: Titans Quarter Boxset

Risking It All: Titans Sin City, Boxset

Hawkeye Series

Here for Me: Volume One

Beg For Me: Volume Two

Printed in Great Britain
by Amazon

63190695R00137